Lazy Prince

Jessica Milk

Contents

Prologue 1

<hr>

A tlas Spiritus Aritiri

8 Days ago

I HATED him. That was the only thought I had of my brother. For eighteen fucking years I hated the lazy prince that I thought my brother was. Hated that he didn't have to work for anything, while I, being the first born, shouldered the royal duties left to us in the wake of our parents death.

That was until three years ago when I felt his pain for the first time on our shared birthday. The day our magic woke and connected us as twins. I felt his soul deep agony that he endured every single day. I suffered with him for the next three years before I ever found out anything about him, except what the current ruling party and Regent wanted me to know.

I found where they kept him six months ago. Found out for the first time that I never had a brother at all. She was always my sister, a sister I never got the chance to meet. A sister whose only protection I could give was a small enchanted earring, crafted by my Quint brother Lucian, that could absorb only the sharpest edge of her pain. This was all I could do for her, except now I found a way. Intent and a sacrifice. I just hope that my Quint brothers understand why I had to do this. I wish more than anything that Valdis could forgive me for not saving her sooner.

Valdis Spyridon Aritiri

8 days ago

The happiest day of my life also ended up being the worst day of my life. My magic woke and my bond with my twin formed. Atlas was okay, more than okay if this bond was to be trusted. He found his Quint and would never know the same lonely fate as me. I could endure this for him. Or so I thought. My magic woke during one of my daily beatings and I killed the guard tasked with breaking me for the day. My magic was much stronger than the Regent was expecting. He sentenced me to be bound by the Iron Coffin to control me, a cursed first born female twin.

The Iron Coffin is made of metal cuffs that are attached individually to every other vertebra in the spine, starting at the top of the shoulders and ending just above the butt. It can only be attached by a Quint, as it requires every type of magic and also an immense level of power. This device does hurt the wearer physically because the metal cuffs are too sharp for the skin to heal over them, so it's always like a gaping wound, but it's designed to injure the soul directly. Shredding its victim from the inside out. The Iron Coffin was banned from every country almost immediately after it was created 400 years ago. It was only used twice before being banned, both victims died within the month of wearing it. I am the only exception. That was three years ago.

Chapter 1: What is that Stupid Tug

Valdis Spyridon Aritiri

7 days ago

My body flew up from the fetal position I always slept in. My heart pounding, ears ringing, veins roaring. Something wasn't right and my body knew before my mind caught up. Something was very, very wrong. But what? Looking around the dark cell carved from the earth I found nothing out of place. The desk where they forced my learning was still neat and tidy. The wooden wardrobe that held the fancy men's clothing, still untouched unless the Regent made me dress up and act like a sleazy prince for the articles. The enchanted ring that disguised me as a boy still wrapped around my left thumb. The Iron Coffin was still fused to my spine. What was wrong? My adrenaline was still spiking and growing more and more as the seconds ticked by. What was the matter? I started to pace my cell on shaky legs, my adrenaline demanded I do something while my muddled brain tried to catch up.

Two eyes? Check. Two legs? Check. Two arms? Check. Pain? Well, that was the easiest one. Double check. Matted white and black hair? Check... Unfortunately, Gods I want a shower. My magic? Check, but it feels a little weird. My twin bond with Atlas... Where is it? Where is he? What's going on? Why can't I feel him? He didn't do it, he couldn't have done it. I started screaming down the bond for him but the only thing that answered was a tsunami of power and it erupted out of me in a storm of plasma, blowing apart the walls of my cage and leaving me in the center of a crater. He did it. Tears streamed down my cheeks falling into the rubble below. Atlas did the ritual. He sacrificed himself for m– Pain shredded my soul causing me to fall to my knees as shouts surrounded me.

"Grab him."

Pain.

"Don't let him escape."

Pain.

"What happened?"

Pain.

"How did he do this?"

Pain.

I knew all their voices but I never knew any of their names, it was another way that the Regent isolated me. Controlled me into whatever they needed or wanted. None of this was new for me except, there was something new. I could see the shapes of their souls. The colors. Their intentions. I knew none of my captors were good people but their souls told me another story, they were the worst kinds of people and they needed to be reaped. With that one thought shining ropes flowed from their souls and reached towards me. My body knew what to do before my mind did as my hand reached out, closed around the strings, and ripped them. Thuds sounded from all around me as lifeless bodies hit the ground, then silence. I reaped their souls.

All twins knew that they were special in this world, because they were gifted by the Gods with extra magic and the ability to share that magic between each other. I know what you're thinking, what stopped twins from killing each other and stealing their magic? If a twins killed one another for their magic then both would lose it and the Gods would curse your bloodline so none of your children would ever be able to wield magic again. But a twin could choose to sacrifice their life and give their magic to their twin. In order for the Gods to determine if the twin truly wished to do this they set up a ritual that must be completed. All twins know this story but the ritual has been lost for many centuries. Or that was true until Atlas.

It was time to go. I didn't know where but anywhere was better than this. Sobs and pain wracked my whole body as I dragged myself up from the rubble and started walking east when an insistent tug halts me in place. I tried once more but the tug pulled me again. I felt for Atlas's bond even though I knew it wouldn't be there. But again I found something new. Four new somethings to be exact. Atlas you brat. He bonded me to his Quint. He fucking bonded me to them. He gave me all of his magic and a Quint bond is made with fucking magic. With nowhere else to go, I turned west and... tug. I turned south, tug. Damn. With a sigh I turned north and started making my way out of the crater.

Maybe this was for the best. Atlas was part of a Quint and all Quint's studied at LAMW. Lustrum Academy of Magic and War was on international soil, gifted to the Headmaster from all five kingdoms. Regent Lukadious couldn't reach me there, he could still hurt me but that was all. Once I was officially enrolled, I was a citizen of LAMW until graduation. Plus it's not like the bond would let me go anywhere else. It needed to be broken and I had to be there in person for that to happen. And, I really wanted to see what Atlas's quint brothers were like. They must be kind if he chose them. Even once the bond was broken I would still be allowed to attend the school as a royal student. I was after all still a prince, well a princess but no one except the Regent knew that.

***

It was official. After three days of walking through the woods with no direction except the occasional TUG, I was going to lose it. The only entertainment I had was the first night, right at midnight, when the Iron Coffin turned on for an hour. My screams kept me company for the hour, and then all of the next day my company was paranoia. I didn't know if it was a fluke or if it was done on purpose. Regent Lukadios may have placed the coffin on my back but he rarely used it and if he did it was only when I needed reminding who held the power. I knew it wasn't a fluke when it happened the next night at the same time and for the same length, and I knew that this would continue until I came back to him and willing became his puppet prince. Without enough time between sessions my soul ached, but I could handle this pain. Years of being beaten forged my will into something unbreakable, and the best part was that Regent Lukadious didn't even know he was doing it.

A figure moving through the woods shook me from my thoughts and plasma was instantly dancing across my arms and flowing through my veins lighting me up from the inside out. I'm sure my purple eyes were glowing brighter than a flash of lightning.

"State your business or I will fry you with over 5,000 volts." My voice came out scratchy with disuse, and damage from years of screaming. A knight wearing my brothers crest emerged from the shadows and stepped towards me. "That's close enough," I took a step backwards. "State your business." My plasma increased in its intensity, lighting up the area around us and showed me the face of my brothers knight. He was a guard at the compound I was kept at, one of the new hires brought in six months ago. He was also the only guards to never take place in one of my beatings. The guard dropped to one knee and bowed his head.

"Atlas sent me. I've co-" My plasma charred the earth in front of him.

"Atlas is dead." My voice broke even more as tears dripped from my chin. "Try to lie to me again and I will kill you."

"I promise you this is no ruse My Prince. Look at my soul and see that I'm telling you the truth." The knight implored and I did just that. His soul was light like the sun but had a hardness to it that showed what I could only explain as a fierce loyalty. I made a noise and he continued. "Atlas sent me to retrieve you once he completed the ritual," the knights voice was thick and I realized that his soul also showed a deep sadness at the loss of my brother. "I was tasked with meeting you on your journey to the Academy, and to help you in any way you may need." The knight looked me up and down, grimacing at my ruddy appearance. "Here," he tossed a bag at me. "A Prince can't walk into the Academy looking like that."

Looking inside the bag I found a finely tailored plaid cream suit. Soft leather oxfords, belt and black turtle neck. There's also some soap, a brush, and some fine jewelry befitting someone of my royal status. "Thank you," my voice came out small. "I didn't really have a plan other than getting onto Academy grounds." My eyes searched the small area looking for anything resembling a puddle so I could clean up the best I can.

"It is my duty now to serve you Prince Valdis. It was Atlas's last wish from me. Please call me Sir Howin." Sir Howin placed a both his fists together in front of his chest in the traditional greeting from the Kingdom of Souls, my home. I returned the gesture in good faith. "Come this way, I saw a stream not far from here." Sir Howin made his was through the brush, me stumbling not far behind him until we came upon the promised stream and I saw to my Princely duties of making myself presentable. The stream wasn't as good as a shower but I made due. It isn't like I was afforded many luxuries in the cage, but that didn't stop me from reading about them in my studies and dreaming of when I could finally use one.

Sir Howin did me a kindness by turning his back to me when I bathed, but he and I both knew that he had already seen the horrors carved into my skin and spine. "There are some Alchemic ointments in the bag, as well as, an enchanted earring from your brother. Both should be able to take some of your discomfort from you. Please let me know if you need any assistance." His soul flared with need, but not a bad need, it felt like he needed to help me in a way so he felt useful.

Walking out of the water and pulling on the cream pants and black oxfords I turned my back to Sir Howin. "I could us some help putting the ointment on." Even though the enchanted ring made sure to conceal my breasts, replacing them with pecs. I still always felt a little exposed without a shirt covering me, but I also didn't want to see the older knights face when he came to the reality of my mistreatment.

His gasp echoed through the trees. "Goddess Valdrestaria, help us." He whispered and then a thud sounded. Looking over my shoulder I saw Sir Howin on his knees, tears in his eyes and fire in his soul. "How could anyone have done this to another living person?" Sir Howin collected himself and walked over the the bag to grab out the ointment and an earring. "Wear this first." He gave me a small golden hoop with a white stone with golden flakes. I gave sir Howin a curious glance but he urged me on. The earring was definitely enchanted and he did say it was to take some pain but how could I be certain? I guess there was one way to find out. I placed the jewelry in my ear and my body sagged to my knees almost immediately, a masculine sob escaping my lips. It has been years since I've felt this good. I'm still hurting but it's finally bearable. My elbows press to the table as more sobs wrack my body. "We will find a way to remove that vile thing from your spine. Mark my words Prince Valdis."

"Thank you Sir Howin." My watery reply makes the older knight smile for the first time since we met.

"Anytime Prince. Now sit up so I can apply the ointment." He gruffs out, and I do as he says presenting my back to him. The ointment goes on smoothly and Sir Howin helps me put on the turtle neck and jacket so I don't get any oil on it. "Brush the tangles from your hair and follow me, the EMC is just through the trees," (Enchanted Motor Carriage). I do just that, running the comb through my curls that spring back almost immediately after brushing. Following Sir Howin out onto the road I find a sleek looking EMC and he opens the back door for me to get in. I slide into to soft leather seat careful to angle my back so the Iron coffin isn't resting directly against the seat. The least amount of pressure put on the Iron Coffin, the least amount of pain it causes me. "The bag to your right has all the school supplies you should need and it has the key accesses to Atlas's accounts. There secured with biometrics but he preassigned you as an admin before he-" Sir Howin's voice catches before he continues. "Before he completed the ritual." He finishes with a hiccup and I realize the old knight is crying, he composes himself quickly and continues. "My direct contact is already in your eCrystal if you need to get in touch with me for anything." He pauses and I can tell that there is more he wants to say or ask.

I give a small sigh and speak. "You may speak freely with me Sir Howin, always." My hand fishes through the leather bag and I pull out a flat crystal, this must be the eCrystal. The screen lights up under my fingers and a hologram of Atlas pops up, my smile brittle a seeing how happy he looked.

"Do you have a plan?" He asks so bluntly and I pause looking through the pictures of Atlas.

"I don't." My voice is small. "My only plan right not is to get onto international soil as soon as possible and break the bond that ties me to Atlas's old Quint. I can't have anyone get mixed up in this royal mess. The Regent needs to answer for what he has done but I-" I take a deep breath and let it all out. "I don't want anyone to know what he did. All the horrible things he let people do to me. I don't want the Kingdoms to know that I a torture little PRINCESS!" The EMC swerves and Sir Howin curses pulling onto the side of the road.

"Princess?" He turns in his seat looking at me. "You've been a Princess this whole time?" My hands slap over my mouth and my eyes look at anything but the first person to show me kindness in years. My whole masculine body trembling in the back seat at the thought of loosing him due to the curse of first born female twins, FBFT. "Show me." His voice comes out like steel and little sparks of plasma erupt across my shoulders and hands. "I will not hurt you Princess, but you must show me your true face."

With a resigned sigh and trembling fingers, I pull the ring from my thumb. The change happens as soon as the ring leaves my skin. Black and white curls fall to my waist. My broad masculine shoulders narrow into a more dainty silhouette. My bust grows, still on the small side though, my hips widen stretching the pantsuit a little. The illusion of a cock disappears but even without taking the ring off, it isn't there it just makes the clothes bulge a little. Luckily my height remains the same, thank the Goddess for being tall. My lips plump a little more than the masculine shape and my jawline softens a little as well. I still look like my twin just feminine. "Now that you've seen that the Aritiri first born is a woman what will you do?" My voice now more feminine, comes out resigned but with more strength than I thought it would. It's been a while since I've taken my ring off, only the

Regent was allowed to see me without it. After a long moment I find the strength to look at Sir Howin.

His deep brown eyes hold mine without pause. The grey strands in his hair shining starkly against his tan skin in the overhead lights of the EMC. Then his soul flares around him, shining like a warm sunset and I know. I know this man. This loyal knight. Would never do anything to cause me harm. Sir Howin unbuckles his harness, steps out of the EMC and rounds to my door. He opens it and then kneels before me, holding his fists together in front of his chest. "I, Sir Howin, do from this day forth. Swear to honor, to serve, to die, to live and to fight for Princess Valdis until my soul has been called by the Goddess Valdrestaria herself. With these words and intent, my servant bond is yours Princess Valdis is you will have me." Swiriling golden magic lights the air between us, a sure sign that the Gods approve of the servants binding that Sir Howin has just handed to me. Holy fuck! Is he for real?

"You would just hand me your soul without even knowing me? Are you insane Sir Howin? How am I to just accept this? We haven't made a contract." Even as I lay this before him he remains steadfast in his position, the glowing magic of the bind still dancing between us. The resolve glowing in his eyes and sunshine soul. "Are you certain?" He simply nods his head. "I, Princess Valdis, accept Sir Howin as my servant from this day forth. This bond will never be able to force him into doing something he truly does not want to do." The glowing magic seal in the shape of a black sun on the palm of my right hand.

Sir Howin rises from his knee, gets back into the EMC and starts driving. "Whatever you decide to do, I will remain your right hand through it all. No matter what. Now get some rest, we will be at LAMW tomorrow evening.

Chapter 2: Can't have a first impression if you're already infamous.

V aldis Spyridon Aritiri

Present

"Princess," a gruff voice pulls me from my sleep. "Princess Valdis, we're about to arrive at the Lustrum Academy of Magic and War. You need to prepare yourself." Sir Howin rumbles from the front of the EMC.

I quickly slide the gold ring back on my left thumb and push myself off my stomach back into a seated position. Making sure there are no creases in my suit and running my hands through my black curls streaked with white, I thank Sir Howin for the warning. Looking out the crystal window my eyes nearly fall out of my head. This place is gigantic. How many building do they need? Well I guess it is an international college so it should be big enough to fit a plethora of students from all five Kingdoms. My busy mind wanders about the giant castle-like buildings with equal parts regular crystal glass and stained crystal glass. They're flower gardens and hedges everywhere. This place screams elite but it also has a homeyness to it too that says "yes we're great but all are welcome".

"Sir Howin," my voice comes out soft with that scratchy quality I don't think I'll ever get rid of. "How many students attend the academy?" Maybe it'll be easier to fly under the radar if there is a bunch of students.

"Roughly 500,000 students attend LAMW but the royal students I think only have about 20 and the I think there are 8 Quints this year." He gives me knowing look from the review mirror. "You won't be able to hide here very long. Incase you forgot, the Regent has been smearing your name for the last three years. Blaming your unruliness' on why Atlas never ascended the throne." He sighs. "We both know that is bullshit but no one else does so I wouldn't expect a warm welcome from anyone. It actually might be easier for you to play the parts the Regent assigned to you in the tabloids."

He pulls into the circle drive of the administration building and opens my door for me. Sir Howin leads me inside and a smartly dressed receptionist almost jumps out of her seat. "Prince Valdis!" She almost screams. "To what does the LAMW owe this pleasure. And we would also like to extend our deepest condolences for your brother."

My hand tugs softly on the earring gifted to me by Atlas. "Thank you for your kindness," my eyes quickly scan the name plate on her desk, "Lottie. I'm here to register for the school year and to also take care of Atlas's personal effects."

Lottie gives me a frown then walks back around to her desk. Her fingers start clicking against a long crystal board and she looks into the screen of another crystal. Sir Howin whispers in my ear that it's and eScreen and the thing she's clicking in is an eBoard. "I'm sorry Prince Valdis, all of Prince Atlas's belongings are still in his room at his Quint house. You would have to get permission from his Quint to enter." She gives me sorrowful eyes over the top of her eScreen. Then she gives me a beaming smile. "I can send them a message if you'd like?"

Shaking my head at her I show her my left hand, she gasps when she sees the black five layered pentagram in the center of my palm marking me as a member of a quint. "When my brother committed the Ritual, he gave me his bond as well as his power. I'd like to put off seeing them as long as possible." She gives me nod, not needing any other confirmation that the gold bond on my skin.

"I can enroll you in classes first if you'd like? That will take us a bit of time since we have to fill a new enrollment form and figure out your class schedule." Lottie say with understanding. I look around the crowding reception area and give her a pleading look.

"Can we do that in a more private area? I'd like to not be gawked at by every student in the school." A small crowd is forming and I'm honestly not ready to play my part of this charade, I'm not even sure I want to play it all. Is playing the part really my best course of action?

Lottie nods her head then picks up her eCrystal and places it against her ear. "Prince Valdis is here and would like to attend the Academy." She nods then stands. "Yes, I'll bring him right now." She turns to me and gestures down the corridor. "Right this way, the Dean would like to enroll you herself." Lottie leads me and Sir Howin down the gothic corridor and stops at a mahogany door before rapping once then entering the office. "Prince Valdis and his knight Sir Howin." Then she turns and leaves.

Standing behind the desk is the tallest woman I've ever seen in my life. Her glowing blue eyes reveal that she's from the Kingdom of Cures and can use both water and alchemy. She's wearing a severe blue pantsuit under a white lab coat. "Good evening Prince Valdis, I'm Dean Whyriss. It is both a pleasure and a shame to have you here under these circumstances." She places her fists together and gives me my kingdoms traditional greeting.

In turn I place my fingers and thumbs together making a triangle in the Kingdom of Cures traditional greeting.

"Thank you for your kind words Dean Whyriss." My expression remains tight. I don't truly understand my feelings about my brother, I know I loved him even though I never got the chance to meet him. When I get a moment later, I'll go through all my feelings. "To what do I owe the pleasure of you taking care of my admittance personally?" I question the severe looking woman. She nods to the chair in front of her carved wooden desk and I take a seat in the soft looking leather. It's hard as a fucking rock. My thoughts jump around my head before I focus back on Dean Whyriss. She gives me a questioning look towards Sir Howin who is posted by the door. "I trust Sir Howin with my life. Anything can be said in his presence."

Dean Whyriss gives a short nod. "Very well then. Lets get started." She pulls out an old tome and slams it on the desk. My whole body tightens to stave off a flinch. "Is it true that Atlas successfully completed the Ritual?" She looks me square in the eyes, daring me to lie to her. At my nod she sighs and continues. "Were there any strange side occurrences when he completed it?"

"A wave of power hit me and burst from my body. I made a sizeable crater in the ground when this happened. Luckily I was taking a stroll when this happened and nobody was hurt." The lie rolls off my tongue easier than I expected it to. Dean Whyriss twitches a little but urges me to continue. "My connection to my quintessence magic also strengthened dramatically, I can now see and touch peoples souls." The Dean looks stunned, the fountain pen dropping to table and rolling slightly before she grabs it.

"We will need to put you through extra lessons until you have a firm grasp on this new level." She mumbles to herself. "Is there anything else that happened?" Dean Whyriss gives me an almost knowing look.

A huge sigh leaves my body and makes my shoulders curl inward. "Atlas also accidentally attached me to his Quint. I can feel all four of them where Atlas used to be." My eyes fall to trace the carving of the wood in the many different swirls of a rising tide. It doesn't feel right to be placed into a bond that belonged to him. They were his family here at the school. "I plan to break the bond." The words fall out of my mouth flat but sure. Silence grasps the whole room as if everyone fears the Gods will come down and smite the whole room. It is Dean Whyriss who breaks the silence first, her voice no more than a whisper.

"Are you absolutely certain about this decision Prince Valdis? Not only is this apparently the will of the Gods but also it is rare for Quints to be formed." She stares at me with saddened eyes and I remember that she is part of one of the most powerful Quint in the world today. "Not to mention that it is apparent that this is what Atlas wanted for you. Why else would he give you his life and his bond?"

A gasp escapes my throat and I shoot forward griping the Dean's desk with all my strength. Plasma sparking across my knuckles and the color of the Dean's soul comes into focus. Blue like the deepest lagoon, and calm ferocity. "It wasn't an accident?" Dean Whyriss shakes her head at me.

"No it wasn't an accident. The Gods would let no such thing happen. Either Atlas gave you everything in the Ritual or he could give you nothing." Dean Whyriss eyes my sparking hands. "Could you please stop charring my wood? It was a gift from my home country."

I snap my hands back to my body so lost in her revelation that I didn't realize that I was letting my magic out to play. She was definitely right to place me into extra lessons. "Sorry ma'am, about the wood and also because it still feels wrong for me to take his Quint. As if I'm trying to replace the hole he left."

The Dean nods in understanding. "Ultimately it is your choice, but until the current norm has changed you will be roomed with his Quint. Mrs. Lottie will escort you to Quint Village. Your class schedule and books will waiting in your room. We have your measurement so that will also be taken care of. Atlas set up all of your accounts before he... passed, so there isn't any more I need from you." We stand at the same time and give each other the proper hand signs from the other country.

Before I head through the door I ask one last question. "Where did they bury him?" I look over my shoulder.

"In the meadows past the school. We have a graveyard where great warriors who fight for the peace of the realm. His Quint asked if he could be buried there and I agreed. It felt like the right place for him to rest." She gives me a sad smile and I wipe a tear from my cheek before heading out the door and meeting Lottie.

"Where would you like to go Prince Valdis? Are you ready to meet your Quint?" She asks in a much to chipper voice.

"I'd like to go to the Warrior's Meadow please." I whisper and Lottie's smile drops into something small.

"Of course." She starts heading east. "Please follow me.

***

The Warriors Meadow is beautiful. Rolling hills with wildflower flowing in to soft breeze only broken by the grid placing of lifelike statues. It doesn't take me long to find Atlas. He looks just like me. Standing there with his eyes closed I almost wait for him to open his eyes and talk to me but the grey stone gives away the lifelessness of the statue. Bubbling anger and hurt swell inside me until I can do nothing with these emotions except pour them from my fingertips into the air. Brilliant white and purple plasma shoot from my hands and spreads into the darkening sky above me. Striking my anger towards the heavens where the Gods reside. My knees give out the same instant my magic does and I crash to the earth. Fat tears watering the grass beneath me. Why couldn't you have found another way Atlas? I would have stayed in that place for an eternity if it meant I could meet you one day. I am not worthy of your sacrifice, I never will be. I don't deserve your Quint. Wiping the grief from my face I steel myself.

Placing my fists together I give my brother the Soul Send, and usher him into the afterlife with peace and love.

"May you have peace in the hands of Goddess Valdrestaria, keeper of souls and decider of death. May your journey be safe and good. May you find rest. Souls be safe." My scratchy voice whispers.

"Souls be safe." A deep rumble repeats from behind me and I see over my shoulder that Sir Howin is saying his final goodbye's with me.

Standing I turn to Lottie, the setting sun lowering behind my brother. "Take me to his Quint, I'm ready to do what I must."

She nods and leads the way.

***

The Quint Village is exactly what it sounds like, except it looks expensive. Like regular sized houses but in the shape of tiny castles. Honestly, it's a little wild but it does convey the great respect the Kingdoms have for their Quints since they do go on to police the realm and fight against malevolence. Lottie takes me right up to the house the backs straight into the woods that surrounds most of the Academy, and knocks. A sudden thought strikes me and I turn to whisper to Sir Howin.

"Is there any type of silencing crystal or enchantment? I require one for my room, also a lock that only opens for me." Sir Howin tilts his head.

"The locks on your door should already be assigned to recognize Atlas's magical signature and since you now hold his magic it will open for you. As for the silencing enchantment," he runs his fingers through his scruffy grey beard in thought, "they're very hard to come by and expensive. The money shouldn't be an issue but the rarity is an issue." He clasps his hands together. "I'll start my search, you have my number but if you can't get a hold of me I'll be in the Academies town a couple miles away. Personal guards are not allowed to attend with their charges."

"Thank you Sir Howin, you've truly been a blessi-" My gratitude gets cut off when the door opens to reveal Atlas's Quint brothers. None of them wear any kind of expression as the tallest one, a man from the Kingdom of Runes as his orange eye color deems, turns to Lottie.

"Thank you Lottie." His deep timbre rumbles through my entire body lighting me up from the inside, "Sir Guard," he nods at Sir Howin, "my brother's and I will take Prince Valdis from here." Orange eyes ushers me inside and I do just that. With a wave at Sir Howin, the door slams shut and nerves shoot up my spine.

Something is very wrong. Danger signals up and down my metal spine and I turn to look at their very familiar faces. Prince Silas Raiden Sunniva, from the Kingdom of Runes. Prince Callum Vanrose Irvine, from the Kingdom of Cures. Prince Kyro Ecicordus Kazetani, from the Kingdom of Flow. And Prince Lucian Vander Kavalyov from the Kingdom of Inditing. They are all the very well know Princes of the other four kingdoms and they are all glaring daggers at me. If looks could kill... damn.

"So, Lazy Prince," Prince Silas glares at me with his glowing orange eyes, "what do you think you're doing?"

He's clearly trying to intimidate me. The only thing intimidating about him is how handsome he is. He's tall with muscles on muscles, short black hair that's cropped closer around his ears, tan skin that shows off the many runes he's burnt into his skin with his Rune magic. His jaw is chiseled to perfection supporting his full kissable lips. Damn he's hot. And hot headed apparently.

"Silas asked you a question." Prince Callum growls out staring down at me. Damn he's hot too. With his glowing blue eyes, wavy blond hair curling around his cut chin, and swimmers build. Gods, I'll be dreaming about him for the rest of my life. He's slightly shorter than Prince Silas but it's not by much. Both of them are still several inches taller than me. "Is he slow?" Prince Callum asks turning towards Prince Lucian, and the biggest of the men steps forward. Of fucking course he's hot too.

He wraps his dark hand around Prince Callum's shoulders and leans close to my face making me squish against the wooden door. His many long black braid, riddled with different charms and crystals, clink together as they roll of his broad shoulders and swing hitting me in the chest and stomach. Glowing green eyes framed by dark lashes search my face before he turns back to Prince Callum and rumbles. "I think he might be." Prince Lucian turns back to me without another word, searching me up and down and finding me lacking. He's absolutely stunning even if he's glaring at me.

A pale hand pushes Prince Lucian aside and Prince Kyro steps forward. Holy Gods in the heavens, he's beautiful. He has a shock of white hair that's gathered in a low ponytail pulled across his shoulder. His slanted glowing gold eyes are full up concern as he steps up to me. "Are you okay Prince Valdis?" He asks as his hand reaches up, is if to touch my face but it falls flat against his side when I flinch back and bump my head against the door. He's only slightly taller than I am as he's the smallest among the four. Prince Kyro's head tilts and I realize my mistake.

I straighten against the door, hardening my stance, face, and hormones. All four of the princes step back giving me the chance to speak. "I'm here to break the bond." I don't meet any of their gazes and continue before any of them can cut me off. "I'm also here to sort his things so if you will excuse me." I go to move between them all but a hand stops me, I fly back as the hand shoves me against the door. Pain slices up my metal spine, healed skin ripping agains the cuffs at the sudden movement. My face remains blank out of habit.

"The fuck you are." Prince Silas growls out. "Looks like we're gonna have a long talk, Lazy Prince, about Royal duties and obligations."

Prince Lucian grabs me by the lapel of my jacket and pulls me from the corridor. This seems like it's going to be a fun talk. Not.

Chapter 3: Royal duties and not so veiled threats

V aldis Spyridon Aritiri

Present

My body is thrown onto the black leather sofa in their common room by Prince Lucian. A fire place sits to my left centered between two sets of glass doors leading directly into the woods behind the house. All the princes surround me on the adjoining couches. Prince Silas paces in front of me absolutely fuming. Like smoke is literally coming off his head. I must have really pissed him off.

"You do realize that Quint bonds are sacred right?" Prince Silas starts. "They are a gift from the Gods themselves. The Gods approve all Quint bonds and they also have to agree when a Quint decides to break them. You can't just decide to break the bond on your own Lazy Prince. That's not how this works." Prince Silas throws his hand around the room gesturing to the other princes. A vein popping out of his neck as he practically shouts at me. "We all have to agree to breaking the Quint and I don't agree."

Prince Kyro leans forward in his chair. "Silas, I thought we agreed when we felt Atlas..." Prince Kyro chokes and Prince Callum places his hand on Kyro's shoulder in support or comfort or something more. I just can't tell with them. "When Atlas preformed the Ritual," he continues giving me a grimace with his glowing gold eyes, "that we would reject any other candidates."

"That was before Atlas chose his brother and the Gods accepted." Prince Silas sighs, his tone softening as he addresses Kyro. A soft broken smile forming on his face. He looks at his other bond mates before turning back to me with his scowl. "We agreed to not take a new member into the bond, but Atlas went ahead and made the Lazy Prince a member, so now we're stuck with him." Silas runs his fingers through is glossy black hair sighing.

Crossing my legs at my ankle I take a deep breath. It's time to start playing this role since they refuse to see me. "Do I get a say in any of this?" My tone comes out as snobby as I can make it. The scratch ever present in my broken voice. Callum and Lucian both give me a sneer so it must be just snobby enough. "I never asked for this." I tell them in case they really don't know if I did or not.

"It doesn't matter if you did or not." Lucian rumbles. "You're here and Atlas isn't. No matter what you may have wanted this is now your responsibility whether you want it or not." Lucian rubs his hand on Callum's thigh. "You will preform the role that Atlas gave you."

Panic starts to creep in. They can't be tied to me. Not when this temporary freedom hangs over me. Not when they will get hurt as collateral because of me. Instead of showing my panic I give a sneer of my own. "You want to be associated with me? Knowing exactly as the public does, that I am the Lazy Prince. Knowing that I will never be able to live up to anything Atlas stood for." I scoff and stand, smoothing the rumpled lapel of my suit jacket. "You want me to pretend to be a good person for what? For my

Kingdom?" I let out a bitter laugh. "For my poor dead parents?" I snort. Sorry mom and dad, I'm sure you both were wonderful people. "For you four." I eye the bewildered expressions on all of their faces. "For Atlas?" I sigh. "I didn't even know him."

"And whose fault is that?" Callum accuses me. Trying to stand and come at me but is restrained by Lucians hand on his thigh. Right, they don't know that Atlas and I couldn't see each other. To them I'm a selfish brat that left my brother with all the responsibilities while I was off having fun and wetting my 'dick'. Gods.

Kyro speaks next his voice coming out stronger than Callum's. "I thought you would have been better than this?" My glowing purple eyes meet his gold and I almost falter. I want to be better than this but I have no idea what the fuck I'm even doing.

"I am who I am." I speak quietly. A thousand meaning under my words but of course they all only see what they have been told to see.

"If you don't preform your duties not only to this bond but to the treaties tied to them, then your life here will be hell." Silas threatens me.

Turning my back on him was clearly the wrong move as instead of looking at the end of a hallway I'm now looking at the ceiling. Pain shoot up and down my metal spine for the second time today and flaming orange eyes come into view. Silas. A burning hand wraps around shoulder sizzling my flesh and effectively holding me down. "So what you mean by hell is that you'll beat me to within an inch of my life and not some three-year-old shit like call me silly names such as the Lazy Prince?" I grit out, no inflection in my voice and my eyes never straying from his. Silas is lucky that I refuse to damage anything that was Atla's, it's the very least I can do for him. But they don't need to know that.

If Silas is shocked by my lack of reaction he doesn't show it. "That's mostly correct Lazy Prince, but you don't deserve the respect of us calling you anything except what you are." His hand is burning through my shirt now the smell of burning wafts between us. Silas must not be able to see or smell through his anger. He's gonna burn me straight to the bone and if the silence from the others isn't indication enough, I'm completely on my own.

"My shirt was imported from the Kingdom of Indicting and was quite expensive." I huff at him snootily. Silas blinks at me then down to where he's trying to burn a hole through my chest and rips his hand back. A muttered fuck coming from his lips. I don't guess he actually meant to burn me but the hard glint in his eyes tells me doesn't actually care. "As fun as this was I need to change my shirt. Can one of you tell me where I'll be staying." I stand surveying the damage to my black turtle neck. Dissapointment flows through me, this was the first item of clothing I had that Regent Lukadious didn't pick out for me and I really liked the shirt. I'll definitely need to get more turtle necks, they feel so secure. Safe.

My gaze slowly filters up to the others when silence continues to remain. All four of them are staring at me like I've said the most ridiculous thing. "What?" I look back down checking that my ring is still on my left thumb. It was. Confusion continues to swim around my head and I give them all a questioning look.

"Are you not in pain?" Kyro asks, his body slowly inching out of his seat. "I could heal you?" His statement sends shock through me as if he would really come over to me and heal my wounds. As if his own bond mate didn't burn me and basically say there was more where that came from.

Looking back down at where I was burnt I see blistered flesh but years of torture and the help of Atlas's earring has me barely feeling anything at all. Wait shit. They can't know anything about that. Think. Think. Think. A lie quickly forms in my head. "I've had worse form jilted lovers and their enraged boyfriends. You didn't think I could be with all those women and not have gotten hurt a time or to by either them or some boyfriend I may or may not have known about." I snort to them shaking my hand in the air at Kyro. "Save your healing on something that actually matters, like my ruined shirt." I can't let him touch me. Healers have the ability to feel all the pain their patient feel to better help them find the source that needs healing. He'll know all the suffering my body has been through and all of this will have been for nothing.

Kyro looks a little offended that I refused him. "There's a healing hot spring in the basement if you would rather use that." He states offhandedly before sitting back in his seat.

"You're fucking weird." Callum states but it's not him my eyes fall to, it's Lucian because he's glaring directly at my earring. Does he know it's enchanted? Can he sense the other two enchantments on my body? But surprisingly he says nothing. "Any shady as hell. Your room is up the stairs and first door on the left." It takes me a minute to realize that Callum was actually helpful in his statement and I turn on my heel, a thanks leaving my lips before I can stop it.

I stop in front of the first door on the left and just stare. The letter "A" is carved into the wood and I feel more out of place than I did before. But when have I ever belonged? Another sigh leaves my lips and I push the door open. The room is nice but has a stale feel to it. It looks like all of Atlas's things have already been moved. A piece of paper on the desk catches my attention and I walk over picking it up.

Valdis,

I know you must have a thousand questions and I'm sorry I can't be there to answer any of them, this was the only way. You deserve more than the life you were given and I hope you take it for yourself. I only ask that you take care of my Quint and save the Kingdom. You don't know this but you weren't tortured because you are a female but because you are the only one who can stop the Regent. I discovered the truth while searching for you. There was a vision on the day of our birth,

"Twins born of royal blood,One granted all,The other granted none,One full of love,The other made of pain,

Once the sacrifice is made,A bond will form,Four soldiers forced,To protect the girl in iron,The coffin of horror,

Listen all to the words of the forgotten,An old God will rise,With help from the Ruler,His dawn is on the horizon,And calamity will strike,

Take heed from these words dear reader,This God was killed for a reason,His bloodline impure,Unbalanced the world will be,If the iron savior hides."

I think the iron savior is you Valdis and I discovered the Regent is trying to figure out how to resurrect an old God. He must be stopped. I know you of all people don't owe the world a damn thing, but I ask that you stop Lukadious.

If you decide to follow this path, all of my things and research is stored in a building, the key is in the desk.

Souls be safe,

Atlas.

The letter crinkles loudly in my hand as I lean heavily against the desk. Deep gasps leave my parted lips. He killed himself so that I would save the world. A world that has done nothing but cause me suffering. A would that gave me pain. A world that put the iron coffin on my back. A world that shreds my soul. The letter goes up in flames but it doesn't matter. The words of the vision burned into my brain. The old Gods were cruel beings that lived for the suffering of the people in the realm. If even one of them were to live, billion would die. I don't care about the billions but Atlas asked me to take care of his Quint and I'll be damned of I fail his final request.

The creak of a floorboard has my head snapping to the right. Like an idiot I forgot to shut my door. Kyro stares at me, his eyes tracking my tears down my cheeks to my hunched form before stopping on the ashes piled on the table. He gives me a sad knowing look before continuing down the hallway without speaking a single word. My body doesn't move before I hear the click of a door down the hallway. I quickly walk over and shut my door. It's good to know the healer is the next door if the constant pain makes me desperate enough. I lean heavily against the door and wipe my face. It looks like I finally have a plan for my future.

Kill the Regent and take my throne, and save the realm if I decide they're worth it in the end. Only time will tell.

In the meantime I have to learn how to hone my abilities, remove the Iron Coffin, and survive my brothers Quint. Easy. Oh, and I also have to pass LAMW.

The clock on the desk captures my attention and I curse to myself. It's 11:15 and I don't have a silencing crystal. A soft curse leaves my lips. How did it get so late? I don't have a game plan for my hour of torture but I know that no one can know. I quickly walk over to the door at the back of my room and thank the Gods when it opens to a balcony right beside a sturdy tree. I climb down as quickly as possible and take off into the woods, checking often to make sure that no one is following me. Why would they suspect the Lazy Prince of sneaking out anyway?

After about 35 minutes of searching at a dead sprint, I find the perfect space to suffer in. Thick trees and foliage cover the area, a stream off to my right. Deciding it can't get much better or private than this I strip the ruined jacket from my shoulders and place it in my mouth. I bit my tongue on the first night and the jacket will taste better and trap sound better than a tree branch will.

The pain starts. Slowly I sink to my knees as the time passes, no longer able to support my weight through the pain. My spine twists at impossible angles trying to alleviate any of the pain I feel but of course it doesn't work. Screams rip from my throat muffled by the jacket and the earth around me. My elbows dig into the earth as my soul feels like it's being electrocuted. When keeping my body from lying on the ground becomes too much work I collapse into the earth. My magic flares arcing from me to the trees surrounding me, my focus on the pain and not my control. If anyone did follow me out here they're surly dead. When it feels like I'm about to die I know it has only been ten minutes since the hour started and I can do nothing but sob into the grass. Please, promises, begging and my dignity fall from my lips in broken scratch raps. No one listens. Eventually no sounds leave me at all, my body as still as the corpse I wish to be. The only reason I know that I live is because my soul is still being shredded and my plasma buzzes in the air.

I try my best to disassociate but I have never lucky enough to break from my reality. Even when I was younger and the Regent touched my body in ways no child should ever be touched.

Once the hour is finally up it takes my mind several minutes to put together that I have suffered no physical pain and am in fact, able to pull myself from the ground. I stumbled into the charred bark of a nearby tree and catch my breath. Why didn't the earring take any of the pain away? My thought run around my head searching for answers. Because it wasn't physical pain. Atlas's didn't know that the Iron Coffin attacked my soul directly and the pain to my physical form was just a "bonus" to the coffin being there at all. I can feel the blood trickle down my back like a thousand spiders from the reopened skin. It never truly heals. Sucking energy into my lungs I push from the tree and begin the walk back to my room.

It takes me an hour before I climb back onto my balcony and collapse on top of the covers of my king sized bed. I can unfortunately only sleep on my stomach thanks to my metal spine. It hurts the least that way. Thank every God that they are black and won't show the blood from wounds I don't have the energy to wrap. My stomach growls reminding me that I haven't eaten in too long but I push the hunger aside. I don't know where the kitchen is and I'm too tired to drag my body from the bed. Nothing matters more to me than escaping into sleep. Hopefully my mind is just as tired as my body and I won't have any dreams at all. I'm never that luck though.

Nightmares about the Regent forcing the Iron Coffin onto my spine slowly morph into old crones screaming prophesies at me about blood, death and sacrifice. About babies being drained and of souls never reaching Goddess Valdrestaria and being funneled into a dark, empty space. About soulless creatures, that look scarily close to human that if it weren't for their decaying flesh, breaking through the earth and killing anything living person. It wouldn't be so bad if it wasn't for the creatures eating the people while they're still screaming at me for help. I don't have the gift of sight, that is an ability only given rarely to the people from the Kingdom of Flow, but I know I'd definitely never want the gift. My own mind is scary enough. Finally the nightmares break and my dream turns towards four deliciously devastating princes and their sinful bodies and piercing eyes.

Chapter 4: Why are there so many stairs?

- -

A soft trill rouses me from dreams that have left me both confused and aroused. Hitting the crystal clock on the night stand beside my bed effectively turns the soft melody off. I'm slowly pulling myself from the bed when a loud blaring alarm comes from wall and the next room over. the sound startles me so bad that I trip out of bed and crash to the floor. I can hear a groan, then a thud, and the alarm turns off. I guess Prince Kyro is a heavy sleeper.

Gathering myself, I stumble into one of the two other doors in my room. The first one I chose is apparently full of the Academies school uniform. Black slacks. Black suit jacket with a gold epaulette to signify my rank in the kingdom. Royals and appointed officials wear gold and everyone else wears silver. My dress shirts range from black to grey to white and even some purple. Nice that we are allowed to wear the colors from our kingdoms but I predict that I will be wearing black for most of my time here. I could probably get away with a dark purple. It wouldn't show my blood as bad as a white one would. Several black oxfords line the shoe rack below. On the other side of the walk in closet are normal clothes for everyday use. A note hangs from on of the hoodies.

I figured you would need some personal items, hope you don't mind.

Souls be safe,

Atlas.

A small smile curls my lips at my brother's thoughtfulness. "Souls be safe." I whisper back to the note, folding it and hiding it in one of the oxfords in the back of the wrack. When I get the chance one day, I'll ask a Rune Master to copy Atlas's handwriting and burn 'souls be safe' into my skin.

Leaving the walk in wardrobe I try the next door and find my initial target. The bathroom. I stop short staring at the greatest creation anyone has ever made and send my gratitude up to Goddess Totalia, the Kingdom of Inditing's Goddess of intentions and creation. The shower. Doing research on the shower was my sole guilty pleasure during my time locked in the cage. When it was time for another tabloid to make its way into the public's eye, I was given a cold bucket of water and soap. I think I cleaned up pretty well for having ten minutes and limited resources, but it was probably due to makeup and editing that I actually looked decent in any of the scandalous photos people "caught" of me.

I strip all of my clothes quickly except for my turtle neck, that, I carefully pry from the dry scabs forming around my iron cuffs. The skin surprisingly doesn't look as bad as I was expecting. Small miracles and all. My thoughts unhelpfully add as I turn the water on for the shower. Whirling back around to look in the mirror I inspect the area on my chest and collar bone where Prince Silas burnt me and note that the skin also looks well healed. It's still red and irritated but it looks way better than it should. Then I remember the small text about bonds that I was forced to learn.

"Not only can a Quint strengthen the magic a bond member can preform, but it can also strengthen one's physical constitution. Quint members have often stated that they can run faster, jump higher, and lift heavier weights after forming a Quint. Bond members have also stated that their groups ability to heal or recovery from significant injuries increased greatly."

Noted.

Shaking the thoughts from my head I jump into the shower and a low groan, that would put many of the companion workers to shame, escapes from my throat. The warm water almost feels sinful against my battered back. My head slowly falls to rest against the smooth black stone of the shower as I soak in the amazing feeling of the water. After too long I set to washing my curly black hair with streaks of white running through it, and my body. Once I'm satisfied that I'm squeaky clean I turn the water off and wrap a fluffy black towel around my waist.

Next order of business is to put on my uniform. I do end up wearing a dark purple button-up and pair the outfit with black oxfords and a black leather belt with gold detailing. My ruined turtle neck goes under my bed until I decide how to discard of it without anyone asking questions. A black leather satchel rests on the door hook in the wardrobe and I sigh in gratitude when I discover that I can just wear it on my shoulder instead of my back. Grabbing the bag Sir Howin gave me when we met, I transfer my eTop and eCrystal. I'll need to check my messages soon but the first order of business if food.

Shutting the door behind me I repeat my role in my head.

You're a Lazy Prince. You're a womanizer. You're a Lazy Prince. You're a womanizer.

I repeat the mantra over and over again until I get downstairs and delicious scents lead me through the common room and into what can only be described as an open plan kitchen. All four of the princes sit around a table meant for five. The fifth seat meant for Atlas. The conversation stops as soon as I walk in the room and I stand frozen in the doorway. They all have plates of food sitting in front of them and my stomach gives a small weak rumble.

Without waiting for invitation I turn to the stoves and quickly make a little to-go sandwich and turn to walk out the door. Just because I'm part of their Quint doesn't mean I have to talk to them. I'm almost to the door when Prince Silas's voice breaks the silence.

"Have a seat." He's obviously talking to me, I'm the only one standing. Turning back to them I eye Atlas's empty chair and shake my head. I will not take his seat. Silas must not have the same reservations that I do since he kicks the chair out a little and barks at me. "Sit down." I catch my flinch before anyone else can clock it and walk to the seat, slowly lowering myself into it. I'm ready for outrage from any of them at me for sitting in Atlas's chair but it doesn't come.

Glancing around the table, none of the Prince's look at me and I decide that eating is more important than whatever game they're playing. Taking a bite out of my to-go breakfast sandwich has a raspy moan leaving my lips and I can literally hear all of the Prince's head snap in my direction. "Fuck sorry." I say around the mouthful I just took. "It's really good." My compliment has Callum blushing and turning away. Ah! Callum cooked the food.

"What is your class schedule for today?" Silas interrupts before I can thank Callum directly for cooking the food. Instead of answering keep chewing and give the flame user a shrug. "Are you being difficult or to you actually not know your class schedule?" Silas pinches the bridge of his nose and takes a calming breath. I notice that Kyro has his hand placed on Kyro's leg, maybe he's helping the hot head stay calm?"

Swallowing my food I give Silas my full attention. "The second one." At my flippant answer, smoke literally rises from the top of his head and Kyro pull his hand from his leg as if it's become too hot for him to touch.

Maybe I shouldn't be pushing his rigid royal buttons first thing in the morning.

"I got here yesterday." I remind him. "Lottie didn't give me packet or anything, she basically dumped me here and said 'good luck' before taking off." I take another bite of my food, chewing eagerly.

"All of that should be in your 'Crystal Ball'." Kyro's voice is soft as he gives me a shy glance from across the table.

I almost choke on my food before swallowing it. "My fucking what?"

"Here," Callum grabs my bag and starts going through my pockets. I'm about to punch him in the face right before he pulls my eCrystal out and starts swiping through it. "It's one of the school apps were asked to download. It's like a student profile that has all the information you'll need. It also has a map that tell you where all your classes and extracurriculars are." Callum turns my screen so I can see what he's doing. And I am again surprised by his helpful attitude. He quickly turns the phone back to Silas. "He's already been put in all the same core classes as us, then he has the usual Quint stuff with us, his required Quintessence and Plasma classes and two private classes." Callum ends on a question looking at the private classes then back at me waiting for an explanation.

"They're precautionary." I look away from his inquisitive glowing blue eyes. "It's to make sure I'm able to control my powers as well as Atlas's." Silence again greets the table. "The Quint made my magic that much stronger too. I'm pretty sure I could power the whole school and still have some magic left over." Sandwich now finished I stare into my hands as if they hold the answers to questions I don't even know how to ask. A low trill sounds around the room and all the guys stand at the same time. Callum shoves my bag into my chest and Lucian grabs the back of my jacket and hauls me to my feet turning me so I'm nose to chest with Silas. He grabs my face and forces me to meet his glowing orange eyes.

"You will preform well in your studies. You will not be tardy. You will not be absent. You will not bring any shame to your brothers name. Do you understand what we will do to you if you fail to do well?" Silas practically growls at me and I nod my head. The position way to familiar the the million times Regent Lukadious held me in the same way before hell was forced upon me. "Say it." Silas shakes me bringing me back to the here and now. Confusion showing in his eyes.

"I understand." I rasp pulling away from them, and securing my bag on my shoulder. Lucian gives me a curious glance before they all file out of the room. Pulling my eCrystal from my bag I quickly glance as my class schedule.

Monday and Wednesday (0800-1700)

Math, History, Languages, Lunch, Plasma, Quintessence, Quint, Extra lessons

Tuesday and Thursday (0800-1700)

Science, Reading, War & Strategy, Lunch, Plasma, Quintessence, Quint, Extra lessons

Friday (0800-1700)

Duties, Government, Politics, Lunch, Plasma, Quintessence, Quint, Extra lessons

My eyes nearly bug out of my head at the hours students in the magic course are expected to pull, but I don't complain, it's better than being beaten. The bulk of my studying will have to be done on the weekends. And I won't be able to get a nap in before I have to make my way into the middle of the woods for my hour of fun.

I walk a pace behind them and follow the princes into the castle where all of our core classes will be held in the north wing. Magic lessons are held in the south wing. The library is the entirety of the east wing. And lastly, all things to do with Quints is held in the west wing.

The crowded corridors part for the princes and they make their way to the stairs with ease, taking them two steps at a time. I try my best to hide me pant after a single flight of stairs and only a couple people give me weird looks. Then the princes do the unthinkable. Ascend another flight of stairs. Then they ascend one more. I feel like my lungs have fallen out of my body by the time I've walked through the door and fallen into the open seat the princes kindly left me.

Who designed this place? My mind rages. Why are there so many stairs? There are another two stories above us. Damn, I need to do some cardio. Silas catches my attention and looks pointedly at his gold watch. I give him a nod letting him know that I know I was almost late to my first class.

The professor breezes into the room and class begins. She doesn't bother introductions and continues where the class left off. Enrolling two weeks late was really gonna kick my ass. Or so I thought.

Apparently I have one thing to thank Regent Lukadious for, my studies, even if he did beat the learning into me. I'm ahead in all aspects of my studies and finally lunch rolls around. As well as climbing four million steps. I just want to talk to the fool that designed this place. That's all I wanna do is talk...

Keeping my distant pace behind the Princes I follow them into the dining hall. It's a beautiful room with long rows of seats and stained crystal glass in the windows and hanging from the ceilings. The Princes choose one of the few tables that only seat five people. They're obviously for Quints. Silas catches my gaze before I can vanish into the crowd. His pointed look at the empty seat lets me know that I'm required to sit with them.

With a little eye roll I saunter over to the chair and sit down with a huff. "You all obviously don't like me." I state in an annoyed voice. "So why do I have to sit with y'all in every class and during meal times?" The question isn't pointed at anyone specific, just to anyone who will answer.

A low rumble answers my question. "Because we're a Quint." Lucian swipes his hand across the crystal in the middle of the table and a screen appears with different meal options. The other three put their orders in and I follow suit. It becomes apparent that Lucians four word answer is all I'm going to get out of him so I shrug and go to ask my question a different way when a feminine voice chimes up.

"Souls be safe." The girl greets me with the traditional greeting and adds the slight bow required when addressing royalty or high ranking officials. I notice she has glowing purple eyes like mine. She's from my Kingdom. Her epaulette detailing is silver on her letting me know that she is of a lower class, but that doesn't matter to me.

I match her traditional with my own giving her a slight bow to show I appreciate her respect. "Souls be safe." I greet her back. "How can I help you?" I give her a soft smile.

"My name is Sinclair, I'm a fifth year here and will be helping Professor Heathrow with you extra lessons." She stands at attention blacking her hand behind her back and her feet shoulder width apart. "Please let me know if you need anything during your time here. It is an honor to meet you Prince Valdis." My magic rears to life causing my eyes to glow more than they naturally do. Sinclair's soul comes into vivid detail. She's strong. Like, really strong. A deep purple comes off her in waves cracked through with a deep yellow.

A true smile forms on my face. "Thank you Sinclair, I am in your hands." I give her another traditional bow and she disappears back into the crowd. Turning back around in my seat I find four gazes back on me. Colors swirl all around the table and I shut my eyes, rubbing them with my hands. An instant headache forming. My earrring warms in my ear and I can fell the pain ebb enough for me to focus on locking my powers back down. These extra lessons couldn't come fast enough. Opening my eyes I focus back on the Princes and they're all giving me shocked looks. "What?"

"You were surprising respectful to that woman?" Callum questions me.

Shit! I forgot to be a duchebag. Being a flirt is so hard. How the fuck do you even flirt?

"Did you not sense her power?" I fake a shiver in my seat. "She'd kick my ass if I tried anything and I like my ass better when it hasn't been beaten." I'll have to apologize to Sinclair the next time I see her and maybe ask for a small favor if she's up to it.

The food arrives on the table and I clap my hands together in a small prayer to the Gods and dig in. Daaaaaammmmmmnnnnn. These chefs really know how to cook. I scarf down my chicken and steamed broccoli in record time. Being sure to use proper table manners so Silas doesn't yell at me. Eye roll. Because the uptight prick totally would. Thankfully, none of the guys comment about how I eat like I've been starved my entire life. I was. Not the point.

The bell tolls and all the guys stand in unison. "You're on your own for the next two classes." Kyro reminds me. "Do you know where you're going?"

"Plasma and then Quintessence," I nod at him. "If I get lost I'll ask someone with glowing purple eyes or someone wearing purple." My smile is a little wiry and I give a stiff shoulder shrug.

"Don't be late or your ass is Silas's." Callum whispers in my ear causing me to flinch away from him and clasp my neck. He just gives me a wink and saunters off after Lucian.

I shake my head and leave heading to the south wing and come face to face with my newest and worst enemy. Stairs. I just wanna talk.

***

Both classes were a bust. The professors only allowed me to do theory work and not actually participate in the lessons until I have been cleared by Sinclair and Professor Heathrow.

The next class if for Quint's only in the west wing, and I have to say, I'm a little excited for it.

I'm the first to arrive and Professor Julia and Alister tell me to head into the men's change room and put on my quint uniform.

If I'm gonna have to change every day I'll need to make sure I'm the first one here or the last.

I quickly head into the men's change room and switch into the black military uniform. Complete with a thousand pockets, over the ankle boots, tight compression turtle neck, button black shirt with my rank and magic classes, and a tactical belt. Kinda bad ass. Can't lie.

I'm just finishing tying my laces when twenty something men walk into the changing room. The four Princes are among the first and they all clock me sitting on the bench tying my laces. It gets rowdy quickly and I see my way out. There are a couple females already waiting and I stand beside them copying their stance. Everyone files out of the changing room and falls into similar stances in neat rows. I can't see the Princes but it doesn't look like we're supposed to be with our Quints yet.

"Form your five and begin!" Professor Julia shouts and chaos explodes.

Chapter 5: Let the pain begin.

Valdis Spyridon Aritiri

Present

I look around as the other Quints quickly for up. There are 2 mixed, 3 all female, and 5 all male quints. 29 males and 21 females if we're counting me as a male that is. Shaking my head I quickly meet the Princes and notice they're all holding hands.

"What are we doing?" I ask standing in the only open spot between Lucian and Silas.

"Pushing power between all of us now grab on." Silas commands and I take a step back away from them.

"I'm not cleared to use my magic yet." I argue instantly, pulling my marked hands towards my body. I'm not given an option to escape when glowing green and orange eyes look to each other then meet my purple ones. They both lunge at me at the same time and grab my hands.

Power roars to life in my veins and my magic answers my distress. Colors race across my eyes and my plasma sparks to life. I barely manage to keep it contained to my own body sparks jumping across my shoulders and buzzing deafeningly in my ears. I can sense all the Quints around us run for cover. Streaks of Plasma arc into the sky above us as my stranglehold on my magic slips. Gritting my teeth I strangle it back down but the sparks still dance across my shoulders.

Professor Julia yell at the Princes to drain my power through our bond and to their credit they manage to a little. I can feel a horrible sucking sensation through our newly formed bonds and my magic decides it very much doesn't like that. Not at all.

This feels so wrong. My Plasma slowly starts creeping down my arms and I know that if it touches Lucian or Silas, I'll fry them. I have to let go. "This is gonna hurt." I mutter out. My magic wants to touch them so bad but it can't. I won't let it. Lucian and Silas grip my hands tighter as if they know what I'm about to do, but they're too late.

My body flies through the air as my magic backlashes against me. I come to a stop when my back slams against the wall twenty feet behind us and my Plasma sparks around me in a violent light show as pain radiates through my metal spine. I collapse onto my stomach pressing my face into the concrete floor beneath me to keep my scream in my throat. Colors swirl around my senses as my fingernails break against the floor, clawing at control. Control over the pain, the plasma, control over anything. My magic agrees with my request and the golden soul cords connect from every living thing in the room and places those lives into my hands. Golden cords wrap around my splayed fingers. I fight against every instinct my body has to keep from making a fist and ripping.

Slowly I feel it. A warmth against my jaw and right ear. Atlas. His earring biting off the sharpest point of my pain. Finally able to catch my breath my magic calms at a snails pace. The soul cords fading away from sight and the buzzing of my Plasma stops. Taking a few more breaths to make sure I'm completely calm, I try to lift from the ground but the pain rears back up.

"Stay down lad and let me heal you first." My eyes meet Professor Alister's glowing gold eyes. His hands glowing with his magic as he reaches for my back.

"No." My voice comes out weak at first and I clear my broken throat. "Don't heal me. It was honestly just a scratch." I force myself to sit up, my face remains a blank mask. Professor Alister reaches for me again and I stand quickly out of his reach.

"You didn't tell Dean Whyriss that you're a Reaper Prince Valdis." Professor Julia says stopping Professor Alister from grabbing me and healing me despite my refusal. I turn a questioning glance on her and tilt my head.

"A Reaper?" My scratchy voice mutters. "I don't understand? I haven't come across that classification in any of my studies." A frown curls my lips downwards.

The four Princes crowd around our small circle making it bigger. I can feel Kyro's intense gaze on me, itching to heal me. Silas want's to yell at me. I can't tell what Lucian wants. And Callum is giddy, like he's found a new toy.

"It's a rare classification. The practice has been lost for some time, but the Academy's memory is long. There should be a tome or two in the library." Professor Julia continues as if the other Princes aren't there. "It will be added to your extra lessons." She turns to the other four Princes. "Prince Valdis will not be permitted to complete a full circle until he has been deemed in complete control by Professor Heathrow and Sinclair. Two person connects should be enough to teach him until that time." She dismisses us and the other Quints file back into their assigned spots.

I'm slow to walk with my group back to our assigned area. I can feel Kyro's and Professor Alister's gaze on me. I give the Professor a smile then turn to Kyro.

"I'll soak in the hot spring when I get home." Kyro again looks upset that I refused his healing once more but I can't let him touch me. He can't know my pain. "You said it has healing properties right?" Kyro gives me a nod then turns away from me. I'm about to speak more when a large hand grabs my shoulder and spins me around.

"What the hell was that?" Silas softly growls in my face. "Why did you let go." His intense gaze searches my face looking for answers.

"I barely have any control of my magic at all. It wanted to hurt y'all and I couldn't let it." I look down. "You all may be dicks, but Atlas wouldn't want any of you hurt." I give him my best shit eating grin and shrug out of his grasp turning towards Lucian. The big man gives me a nod and I walk to him. Minerals neutralizes Plasma, he's the safest option for my magic and he knows it.

Professor Julia hovers nearby as I place my light palms into his dark ones. Lucian refuses to meet my eyes as we let the magic build between us. Instead he glares at my earring.

Once our magic becomes familiar with one another. Anytime my magic tries to take over the connection, Lucian's magic lashes out and leashes mine. Big man is really walking my magic like a dog. A slight zap rings through my body at the thought and a grin takes over my face. Lucian smiles too as if he knows exactly what happened, then he's quickly back to glaring at my earring.

"Good." Professor Julia comments, "Now focus on conjuring a shield around the three of us." She commands and I close my eyes focusing on that and the feel of Lucians magic. His magic feels steady and firm but also flowing, like carved marble or shaping metal. Professor Julia's clap makes me open my eyes and around the three of us is a warped glass dome.

Professor Julia flicks it with her finger and shimmering green and purple magic ripples out from where she struck. "A+." She smiles. "That's a very nice shield."

Lucian's magic slowly nudges my magic back into my body, showing me how to pull it back then he lets go of my hands and steps back. Braids clinking together as he walks towards the changing room.

The bell trills and Professor Alister calls time for class. "Prince Valdis." He calls as I head for the changing room. "Hang back, Professor Heathrow and Sinclair decided your lessons were best done here since you have more magic than expected." I nod and stand beside him.

Professor Heathrow and Sinclair walk in as most of the other students leave, the only ones to hand back are three of the Princes. Kyro noticeably absent.

"Souls be safe." Sinclair greets in the traditional greeting. I greet her back and she intoduces to Professor Heathrow. He greets me then his colleagues before they leave the room he then turns to the other Princes.

"I apologize Princes, but this will be a closed lesson until further notice." Callum looks disappointed, Lucian doesn't seem to care and Silas goes to argue but Professor Heathrow cuts him off. "If Prince Valdis is a Reaper, then it is tradition for the lessons to be private between our people." The three Princes nod and leave the room.

"Is that true?" I ask Professor Heathrow.

"It is." He gives me a sad look. "Reapers are only created through intense pain and the completion of a successful Ritual." He looks me up and down. Sees the way I am ready to run and continues to speak. "I will not ask for your story but know that your soul will tell me your pain." He sits on the ground and Sinclair does the same. "Are you ready to begin? Anything that happens can never be spoken of outside of the three of us."

I take my seat so we're sitting in a triangle. "What do I do?"

"First you will need to look within and open your soul to us." Sinclair speaks. "It will feel uncomfortable at first Prince Valdis, but soon it will feel as comfortable as breathing." She takes a deep breath and then I can feel her soul reaching for mine.

It takes me a minute but I eventually reach back and Sinclair gasps her head snapping towards Professor Heathrow.

"Yes I feel it Sinclair." He addresses her then looks back at me. "No Reaper in our history has ever been male, and it looks like you will not be the first. Princess Valdis." It should feel like a threat that they both know my secret but it doesn't. Just as they are reading my soul, I too am reading theirs and I feel no threat. Only comfort. They will not share my secret. They can't. Loyalty written into their very beings.

"What comes next?" My scratchy come out soft, soothed by their souls.

"Read." They say at the same time and that's all I can do when they throw their souls at me.

An hour passes before I know it and the three of us have tears rolling off of our chins.

"Now we will all connect hands and you will call on your Plasma. Feel it, play with it, get to know it. This is your next task." Professor Heathrow instructs.

"Won't I hurt you?" I'm reminded of earlier today.

"You won't." Sinclair states taking my hand. "We know how to ground your magic. The full circle lets it expand so you can feel it but the magic never truly leaves you. We act as an extension to you, like a wire." I nod at her explanation and complete the circle by grabbing Professor Heathrow's hand.

We spend an hour like that. Getting to know my magic.

***

My body feels lighter on my walk back to the house. I'll have to continue to work on my control but it's nice to be able to connect with my magic. I wasn't allowed to do that under the Regent's control.

Seeing the house in the distance my strides slow. I'm not ready to see any of the Princes. They're not as rude as they could be but I still don't enjoy the feeling of not being wanted and having no where else to go. Instead of heading to the front door I turn east and walk to the Warrior's Meadow instead.

Finding Atlas, I sit with my legs crossed and place my knuckles against one another and close my eyes. Professor Heathrow and Sinclair showed me the art of meditation and I'm not quite ready to let the feeling go. It's one of the few things I can share with Atlas now that he's no longer with the living. My soul.

It's the darkening sky and cold raindrops that pull me from my serene state. "Souls be safe." I say to His statue before heading back to the house.

I'm soaked to the bone by the time I walk through the front door and am immediately accosted by the four Princes.

"Where have you been?" Silas questions. "Your lessons ended at five, you should have been here an two hours ago." He walks prowls forward causing me back into the closed door. The foyer crowding with blue, green, yellow and orange.

"I was with-"

"With a whore?" Callum questions turning towards Lucian. "I was right, you owe me ten credits." His grin is undeniable.

"No, I went to see-"

"Why are you wet?" Silas leans in closer and when I give him an 'are you serious' look, he seers at me. "It doesn't matter. You are to come straight back to the house after every lesson. Do you understand?" He gives me an expectant look. It's understandable when I haven't fought him on any of the rules he's placed before me, until now.

"No." I stare him directly in the eye. "I will do what I want with my free time." I bump shoulders with Silas when I walk past him. "Since it's mine." I snarl and round the corner heading up the stairs. It's Kyro's soft voice that halt me mid-step, causing me to turn around and head down the stairs instead.

"You promised to get in the healing springs when you got home." He rings his hands around the sleeves of his uniform jacket and I want to reach out and grasp his hands to stop him from figiting. Instead I speak.

"Thank you for reminding me." My concession tilts his lips up slightly and he steps in front of me. Leading me down a separate hallway and down stone stairs. A gasp escapes my lips at the beauty of the room just under our house.

Artificial lights give the room a soft yellow glow. A deep pool is carved out different colored crystals in the middle of the room. Fluffy black towels are placed on wooden racks on the back wall and robes hang beside them.

Kyro gives me an expectant look, he wants to see my injuries.

"I think I can manage to soak in the springs on my own. Thanks but I'd really rather not get naked in front of a dude I just me." I snark at him and a frown tilts his plump lips down again. "If you're feeling some kind of guilt or pity, that's your business. Don't make it mine. I have enough to deal with." Kyro gives me a single nod before turning his back to me and walking away. It hurts more to push him away than I thought it would. I'm rubbing at my chest absently when he pauses at the door looking over his shoulder. White hair flowing like a waterfall down his back. His glowing gold eyes clock my hand over my heart and I slowly lower it.

"You missed dinner, Callum left you some food." That's all Kyro says and then he's gone through the door.

My head drops and I stare down at my marked palms. A black sun on the left, layered pentagram on the right.

What am I doing? Why am I rolling over for these men? I know my spine is made out of metal but it feels like I don't have a spine at all.

That's enough thoughts for now. I strip my clothes noticing the many holes poking through the back of my dress shirt where the Iron Coffin tore through it. I'll have to order some heavy duty turtle necks to I don't wear through all my shirts too quickly. Grabbing my eCrystal from the pocket of my slacks, I look up where to order the clothes then punch in the house location. I send a silent thanks to Sir Howin and Atlas for setting up my accounts beforehand.

That taken care of I slowly lower myself into the springs and a long groan full of pleasure falls from my throat. The springs healing properties taking affect instantly. I could get way too used to this too fast. I'll have to limit the use of the springs. I'm way too exposed in here. The steam helps but it won't be able to hide the metal in my spine, and may only slightly concertgoer the fact that I don't have a dick.

I run my hands down my masculine chest and over all the wounds I can reach to help the water heal my wounds quicker. The process goes smoothly until I get to my back and can't reach. I would float but the metal makes me sink if I don't work to remain floating. Instead I prop myself up against the edge and soak. The skin will never truly heal but that dosn't change the fact that this is the best I've felt in my entire life.

A heartbroken sigh leaves my lips when I pull myself from the water and wrap a robe around myself. I tuck my dress shirt and eCrystal into the robes pocket and throw the rest of the clothes into the dirty hamper.

I quietly creep from the springs back upstairs into the kitchen. There's a covered plate sitting on the counter and I decide reheating the food is too much work for hungry stomach and dig in. A whispered thanks to Callum leaves my lips.

"You're welcome." He whispers back in my ear. I flinch so hard I hit my elbow on the counter. "Fuck!" I spin around coming inches from Callum's face where he's leaning down to whisper to me. "Stop doing that." I say rubbing my elbow and leaning back away from his face. The counter keep me from being able to actually take a step back.

"I can't help myself." Callum places his hands on either side of my hips. "Your reactions are so fun." He says in a low voice. "And I enjoy the way you eat my food."

"How do I eat your food?" I ask scoffing at him. "Like a normal fucking person?" My pulse skyrockets at his nearness, my blood heating and hidden lady parts waking up.

"Like you're making love to it."

Oh. Oh. Is he flirting? OMGods he is.

"No I don't." I look anywhere but at his glowing blue gaze. A blush staining my cheeks.

"Yes you do." He finally leans back away from me and grabs a glass from the cupboard. He fills it with water then holds it out to me. "Thirsty?"

"Yes." Wait. "I mean no!" I say quickly, my blush spreading further. Callum laughs then grabs my hand, placing the glass in my hand. He says good-night with a wink then leaves the kitchen.

I gulp the water down deciding that I've had enough people for today. Fuck.

I go to my room and study until it's time to go into the woods for my hour of fun.

Chapter 6: Wolves are not sheep.

‑‑

Silas Raiden Sunniva

Four days later.

He's absolutely nothing like the tabloids say he is. They called him a flirt. The called him lazy. They basically said he was a wild child who cared for no one except himself.

That's not what I see in him at all. He's respectful. Studies harder than even me. And he's excelling in his private lessons. He hasn't done anything to give me a reason to hate him except him being here at all. That pisses me off even more.

Atlas should be here. Not him.

Valdis is constantly pushing us away. Keeping us at arm distance. All four of us. I'm greatful that he isn't trying to replace Atlas but it just makes me hate him more that he's being a decent person. And I hate myself for wanting to hate him.

It doesn't help that he's just as pretty as his brother, maybe even prettier.

I finish getting dressed for today. I make sure there are no wrinkles in my uniform and head into the kitchen where Callum has made us breakfast. He enjoys mixing he Alchemic talents and cooking, always adding extra things into his meals to give our bodies the extra nutrition that they need.

I tuck Kyro's white hair behind his ear and kiss him on the cheek before sitting down in my seat. Callum sets a plate in front of me and winks before doing the same for Lucian. The big guy sits in his chair with a heavy thud. He tilts his head back when Callum wraps his hand in his long braids and pulls his head back. Callum slants his lips across Lucian's and the big guy smiles and complies. They look so good together. My magic heats my blood and I devour the two of them with my glowing gaze.

Most of the other Quints have lovers outside of their bonds but I find that no one can compare to my Quint brothers. Orange, gold, green, and blue. Purple used to be part of this love but Atlas is gone, taking a piece of me with him.

We all finish our meals quickly and head out the door. It's not till we're in our seats for class that I notice a certain Prince isn't with us.

"Where is he?" I whisper into Lucians ear and the big guy gives me shrug. Of all the classes the Lazy Prince could have missed, this was the wrong one.

It is a Princes duty to know what is expected of him and how he can best lead his people.

An orange haze coats my vision. I'm pissed. Lucian and Kyro scoot away from me slightly to protect themselves from the heat my body is giving off.

Don't kill him. Don't kill him. Don't kill him.

I chant to myself. It's time to finally teach the brat a lesson.

Chapter 7: Sheep are not wolves.

Valdis Spyridon Aritiri

Four days later.

My face Slams against the side of Academy. It's a jarring experience, especially when you're not expecting it. The building is softer then most of the guards boots though so I take it like a champ. My head is pulled back by my white and black curls and my face is slammed into the Academy again.

Don't kill him. Don't kill him. Don't kill him.

My magic pouts and I'm suddenly staring at the blue sky. Silas's Orange eyes come into view. It looks like he's done pretending he doesn't want to hurt me.

"You remember when I told you there would be consequences for breaking the rules right?" He asks as he pulls me off the ground by the lapels of my uniform. He shoves me into Lucians arms and the big guy holds me up. I nod my head at him. "Tell me Lazy Prince, why are you being punished?" Silas growls the question at me.

"I was absent for the first class." I rasp out. Continuous nights subjected to the Iron Coffin is tearing my body apart from the inside out and I slept through my alarm because of it. Silas confirms my answer by punching me in the gut and I double over making no sound. Lucian keeping me from falling to the ground. Silas leans down to my ear.

"Are you going to miss a class again?" He questions. When I shake my head he punches me in the gut again, Lucian lets go causing me to fall to the ground. "See that you don't. I'd hate to break your pretty face again."

He's probably extra pissed because I miss our class 'Duties". He's such a stiff. All royal students and high ranking officials have these bogus classes on Fridays. I tilt my head backwards looking between Lucian's legs and see the other two Princes. Kyro won't look at me. Callum is frowning. Neither of them make any move to stop our other bond mates and a sigh leaves my lips. I can feel Lucias looking at me, his gaze moves to my ear and I can feel him glare when Atlas's earring heats and bites part of my pain off. When I don't move to get up Silas snarls and storms off. The other three following behind him. I wonder how long it will take for the others to join Silas in hurting me too.

Thank Gods it's Friday and I can leave campus and meet up with Sir Howin in the college town a couple miles over. We really need to go through all of Atlas's research. I want to nail Regent Lukadious before my 22nd birthday in four months, when I'm eligible to ascend the throne. I don't know how long it's going to take for him to figure out where I am and the waiting is making me twitchy.

Classes are done for the day. The weekend ours to do with as we please.

I don't bother heading to the house, instead I head to the front gate. Sir Howin already waiting in a sleek EMC. I flop into the passenger seat and rattle the location of the house to him. He nods and we take off.

Twenty minutes later we stop the EMC out side a medium sized cabin in the woods outside of the college town. I get out first and walk to the door putting the key into lock and turning. The sound of several locks turning sounds and I push the door open. Boxes line the every available counter and I pull the lid off the closest one, documents are inside. Sir Howin comes up beside me and peers into the box over my shoulder then looks around the room.

"We're going to need some help Princess. Is there anyone you trust?" He asks looking into my eyes. "Maybe your Quint?" He adds.

"No." I say immediately. "The less people that know, the better." I turn away from him and pace. "But." I start pausing my forward and back walk. "There might be one." I say and pull my eCrystal from my pocket and place it against my ear. The person on the other line answers on the first ring. "Are you alone?" I ask and a 'yes' answers me back. "If your Prince asks you for a favor what would your answer be?"

"Where do you need me?" The voice asks and I send them the location.

A knock sounds on the door thirty minutes later and I open the door to reveal Sinclair. "Thank you for coming. Let's get to work." I say ushering Sinclair into the room. She greets Sir Howin traditionally and looks around the room.

"It's good to see you again Sir Howin." Sinclair says and in turn he ruffles her hair and grins. Turning to me she asks. "What do you need from me?" She asks and I explain to her everything that Regent Lukadious has done to me. Her eyes are glowing intensely when I've finished and she asks one question. "Why not just come forward and let the people know what he has done?"

I turn away from her. "I will if we can't find any other way to take him down but if it can be avoided. I would rather no one know about this."

I guesture to my whole self. "I don't want anyone to know how weak he has made me." My gaze finds the floor and stays there. "I also don't really understand what his plan is. Why he did this to me. It can't have been just because I'm a first born female twin. Where do I fall into this?"

A hand finds my shoulder and a different hand finds my other shoulder. "Of course Princess." Sir Howin says.

"We will figure this out. Let's get started." Sinclair grabs the closest box to her and sits down on the dusty couch. Sir Howin follows suit and I do the same.

That's how we spend the next day and a half. Sinclair and Sir Howin leave in shifts to bring back food and toiletries. Luckily the bathroom in the cabin is working. I of course find a little hidey-hole from the hours of twelve to one am to be tortured in privacy. During our little exploration we found documents in every room except the basement, that's where all of Atlas's belongs are. I decided to go through them at another time.

We've collectively made our way through twenty boxes tracking Regent Lukadious spendings of the Royal funds, trying to find anything suspicious. The work is tedious and frustrating but worth it. Or it will be when I can execute him for treason.

It's Sunday afternoon when I decide we're getting nowhere fast and call time.

"I think that's enough for now." I rasp out. "My eyeballs feel like they're bleeding." I rub my eyes with the back of my hands.

"Thank the Gods." Sinclair shouts. "I've read the same line at least five times." She stands and stretches like a cat. She looks at her watch and turns glowing purple eyes to me. "I'm heading back to the academy, want a lift?" She questions. Sir Howin speaks before I can.

"That's a great idea. I was planning on looking through a couple more boxes before grabbing my things from the Inn." He doesn't look up from the paper he's reading. "I think I'll stay here and keep an eye on the place." He sips his tea before continuing his work, muttering to himself under his breath.

I stand beside Sinclair and look down at her. She's slightly shorter than my 5'11' frame. I'm six foot in shoes and I mentally shake my fist at the Gods for not giving me one more inch.

That's what he said. Lol.

"Lead the way." I say to her and she heads out the front door. I leave the house key on the coffee table and follow her out. I slide into the leather seat of her EMC, it's much boxier than Sir Howin. It almost has a military feel to it. Sinclair answer my unasked question.

"It's a military model. Reinforced glass and frame. Nothing short of a mountain collapsing could break my baby." She gives a vicious smile. "All terrain travel and the magic mileage is pretty decent. I just have to recharge it every 400 miles or so."

"Why?" It's the only thing I can ask as I gesture to the whole EMC.

Sinclair lets out a hearty laugh. "My dad." She answers simply. "He used to be a high ranking official in your dad, the true King's, army. Major Kairos, Commander of the Soul Knights, couldn't have me drive anything less than battle-class." She shrugs and rubs the steering wheel affectionately. "Don't tell him but I honestly love Tardigrade. That's her name."

"Like the micro-animal?" I question and she nods her head. "Cool."

"My father was demoted when Regent Lukadious took over after the King and Queen passed. We've been doing well but that's why my epaluttes are silver instead of gold even though I'm in the Friday classes."

It makes sense. She has the power, her glowing purple eyes a status symbol all on their own.

"Are you only being kind to me because I can help your family?" The question rolls off my tongue before I can stop it. It is a fair question though.

"No." She instantly. "I mean, it would be nice." She continues. "But I'm not expecting a reward. My father taught me to do the right thing. To look beyond what everyone else says is normal. To find my own answers." She looks over at me then focuses back on the road. "I knew you weren't what everyone said from the moment you greeted me back in the dining hall." She smiles. "I'm glad. You're actually pretty cool, cool enough to be my friend."

We both side eye each other and then bust out laughing. "Friends." I agree once our laughter gets under control. "Can I ask a favor?"

"Of course."

"Can you pretend to be my girlfriend?" I eye her nervously. It's kinda a big ask. I ramble on before she has the chance to speak. "I'm supposed to be this playboy Prince but I suck at flirting. Plus people are going to wonder why we are together so often. It can also be helpful for when we're gone for the whole weekend committing treason. It'll also put you on a direct path for either my Quint's wrath or Regent Lukadious or even both. You know, if you still want to help me?" I peek a glance over at her and see she's fighting demons trying to contain her laugh. "Don't laugh." I wine.

She does in fact. She laughs her damn lungs out. "Yeah, we can fake date." She looks over. "It might actually get me real date if the boys get jealous." She shrugs her shoulders. "Plus being Major Kairos's daughter already puts me in the line of fire. It's nothing I'm not used to." She grins as we pull into the school gates. "This might actually be fun. And are you really even friends if everybody doesn't think you're secretly dating?" She raises her eyebrow at me.

She parks and lets out a gasp twisting in the seat to face me. "What are our pet names for each other. They have to be kinda horrible right?" She places her hand on her chin deep in thought. "I'll call you 'pumpkin' and you'll call me 'muffi'-"

"Wait wait." I cut her off quickly. "Everybody will probably start calling us by those names and I don't think I'll be able to keep myself from throwing up if someone actually calls me 'pumpkin'." I tell her with my most serious face to make sure she knows I mean business. "How about I call you Sin, and you call me Val. We can mix a couple 'babes' in there to really sell it. Sound good?" She nods to that.

"PDA?" Sin goes on. "How far are we comfortable with? I'm okay with touch as long as it's respectful. Cheek kisses are okay too, maybe an actual kiss if we really need to sell it." She tilts her head. "That work for you?"

"Yeah I think that will work. I don't see us needing to do anything big. One public cheek kiss and the whole academy will be talking about it." I hold my hand out to Sin. "Let the games begin babe." She laughs and places her palm in mine.

"See you later babe." I get out of the car first and walk around Tardigrade and open her door for her. We separate with me kissing her cheek and I head home.

Trepidation creeps up my spine when I walk through the front door. My senses going on high alert. I figure out the reason when I walk past the living room. All the Prince's are waiting, standing around the room.

"Where have you been?" Silas asks in a clam voice. Shivers run up and down my metal spine.

Danger.

"That's none of your business." I state, inching out of the room.

Silas nods and Kyro winces trying to catch my eye but I don't connect. "Looks like we're doing this the hard way."

Arms grab my body and pull my head back by my hair. When I go to shout, vile tasting liquid is poured into my mouth. A hand covers it before I can spit it out.

"Swallow." Callum commands. A hard glint in his eyes. I have no choice. Either I swallow or suffocate. I swallow. "Good boy." Callum purrs removing his hand from my mouth.

Silas strides over. "How long until it takes effect?"

"Any second." Callum smirks.

Silas nods. Lucian drags my body over to a chair and throws me into it. His hands bracket my shoulders from behind before I can make a run for it.

What the fuck did Callum just give me?

Panic creeps in. The only sign that I'm starting to freak out is the slight increase in my breathing.

"Where were you doing this weekend?" Silas questions.

When I don't respond pain sears my throat. "I was on the moon." I spit the lie at him and the pain doubles.

They gave me a truth potion. I didn't even know Callum's skill was advanced enough to make them. Only fifth years learn how to make.

"The pain won't go away until you tell the truth." Callum, the Prince from the Kingdom of Cures, smiles at me. Glowing blue eyes study me. Water is the Kingdom of Cures' primary magic, for the lucky few who have the glowing blue eyes, they have the secondary magic, Alchemy.

"I was in a cabin." The truth slides from my lips and the pain lessens.

"Who were you with." Silas asks.

"Sinclair." The half truth slides out and the potion accept the answer. It is the truth but it's not all of it. Silas is being to vague.

"What were the two of you doing." He fires off another question.

"A gentleman doesn't kiss and tell." Lucian's grip tightens and Callum scowls at me. The pain in my throat roars to life again.

"I asked what you were doing."

"We were hanging out, reading, eating." I give him a smirk, licking my lips. The potion accepts my vague answer.

"You two dating or something?" Callum blurts out. This is probably the easiest question to answer.

"We have an agreement." I leave the statement as is. Let them come to their own conclusions.

"What else are you hiding?" Silas's glowing orange eyes scrutinize me.

The pain triples but I keep my mouth closed. Those are my secrets, not the Princes. The question was vague but I have the strongest answers to them causing the intense pain.

My body is rigid as I fight the potions. Liquid starts to collect in my mouth and throat causing me to cough, blood dribbles from my chin. The copper taste filling my mouth. My gaze remains on Silas, refusing to answer.

Hands grip my jaw tilting it back and squeezing my cheeks against my teething causing my mouth to open. "Fuck." Callum mumbles, looking closer inside my mouth. "That's not supposed to happen." I try to rip his hands away from my face but Lucian catches both of my wrists and holds them behind my back with one hand. His other hand fists back into my hair tilting my head back farther. Callum's fingers reach into my mouth and push my tongue down. I fight back a gag. "Good boy." Callum says absently as he inspects my throat.

This would be so hot if the circumstances were different. I hate to admit that my lady bits are totally awake at Callum's and Lucian's double team, but they are and I'm soaked.

"Fuck. Answer Silas's question now." Callum says, panic flooding his whole body. "Do it now. You're going to burn a hole in your throat." Callum says in a rush. I may not know him well but I believe him. His panic too real to fake. Plus it definitely feels like a hole is being burned in my throat. My gaze lands on his and I hold his glowing blue eyes.

"No." Lucian's grip in my hair becomes punishing, it helps distract me from my throat. Atlas's earring not doing much to cut out some of the pain.

"Fuck." Callum's panic is so real I can practically taste it through the blood. "Silas take back your question." He quickly to Silas. "Do it quickly."

I know Silas's answer before he says it. "No."

Callum steps away from me and runs into the kitchen. He comes back seconds later with different herbs a grinder and a pot with water in it. He starts throwing things together and blue magic lights his hands through the process.

Lucian allows me to lean forward and I cough blood onto my pants. There's a small puddle when Callum finishes. He runs over to me and hands the new potion out to me.

"No." It' the only thing I'm able to croak out and Callum frowns looking at the potion, understanding lights his face before determination takes it over.

"You're going to drink it right the fuck now." He lunges forward and my jaw is pried open again. I swallow. The relief is almost instant. "Kyro." Callum calls and the white haired Prince is there.

I shove to my feet with more strength than I knew I had. "I think you've all done enough." I glare at them all and race up the stairs before anyone can stop me.

Silas was really going to let a hole burn through my throat.

I rub the skin on my neck and lean heavily against my locked door. Slowly I sink down and wrap my arms around my knees.

I'm not safe here either am I?

Chapter 8: Avoid your Problems.

Valdis Spyridon Aritiri

Present

Kyro corners me in the woods on my walk back after my Extra Lessons Wednesday afternoon.

"Why won't you let me heal you?" He asks me point blank. Golden gaze blazing. I look around the foliage searching for the other Princes. Kyro lets out a sigh. "It's just me, I'm alone."

I nod and step around him. "Why should you waste your magic on me. It's not like any of you actually care about my well being." I say flippantly. He jogs up to me and cuts me off.

"It's more than that." He stares at his hands, the five layered pentagram on his left palm. "You actively avoid my touch."

"No I don't." I scoff. When I try to step around him again he reaches his hand out to grab me and I jump back.

"You do." He gives me a bland look and I run my hand through my short curls.

"Look." I start already hating myself for what I'm about to say. "I'm not here because I want to be." Kyro flinches at my words. "I'm here because I was forced into a bond I never wanted. I'm here because you all would rather torture me than let me go. All of you think I caused Atlas's death. News flash Kyro. I had no part in his decision. I wasn't even there. I never would have let him go through with it. " I rub a hand against my face. "It would hurt more if the person healing me, hated me." The Iron Coffin can't be healed and I'd rather not face the disappointment. "I have enough to deal with." My shoulders drop, feeling the weight of everything.

I step past him, but freeze at Kyro's hateful words. "Of course you weren't there. You were never there when he needed you." The venom in his words poison me. Reminding me of why I wasn't there. Why I couldn't be there. I spin around and face him ready to shout but instead.

"Where were you?" I whisper the question to him. Tears fill his eyes and he looks down.

"We didn't know." He whispers back.

"Then how could I?" I don't wait for an answer. Instead I turn my back and head home. I ignore the others and head straight upstairs.

Once I'm in my room I strip out of my uniform except for the sleeveless turtle neck, boxers, and socks. I throw on a black sweat set and open my window. I sit at my desk and pull out my assignments and get started before my body demands sleep. I'm in the middle of a paper for War & Strategy when I feel it.

The Bond.

The Quint bond has been intact long enough for the connections to form. I can feel them. All four of them. And it's not the vague sense I had of them earlier. It's a tsunami of emotion, confusing and overwhelming.

If I can feel them they can feel me.

Nope. I shut that shit down at lightning speed and lock it up tighter than my metal spine. Anger. Grief. Disapproval. And curiosity are the last four emotions I feel before it's gone.

An angry pounding sounds on my door moments later and I swing out of my seat. I unlock the door and rip it open blocking the doorway. They aren't welcome in here.

"The connection finally forms and you immediately shut us out?" Silas question's with anger. I obviously know which of the four emotions was his. I'm a little shocked to see Lucian behind him.

"Bonds aren't meant to be closed." Lucian rumbles. I think his emotion was disapproval.

"You don't get to tell me how to exist in a Quint I don't want to be part of." I slam the door in their faces locking it. I really don't have the energy for their shit right now.

"You don't get a choice." Silas shouts through the wood.

"When have I ever?" I rasp under my breath turning back to my desk to finish my paper. The realm may see me as many things, but I will not be seen as stupid.

***

I shoot up in bed. A weird alarm sounding from around the room.

"All students meet in the west wing." A monotone voice sounds out. The message repeating every few seconds.

I throw on a fresh black sweat set and slip into some running shoes. I open my door and quickly jog down the stairs meeting the Quint at the front door. I don't look at any of them and we walk to the west wing. It's the only place big enough for all the students. I see Sinclair's gold hair piled in a messy bun on her head.

"Sin! Babe!" I shout in the crowd. She turns and makes her way to me. I loop my arm around her waist and pull her close to my body to shield her from the crowd. I can feel all of the Prince's staring at us.

"Val." She sighs and melts slightly in my grasp. "I've been looking everywhere for you."

"Do you know what's going on?" I question noticing for the first time that she wearing a very small nightgown. They're pink with yellow ducks all over it, booty shorts and matching crop top. I bite my lip looking at her trying not to laugh. That's a cute fucking nightgown.

She notices my gaze and looks down. "I wasn't expecting company." She blushes and the laugh slips from my lips.

"Do you want my hoodie?" I start shrugging out of it when she turns and presses her back against my front stopping me mid motion.

"No." She tilts her head back and looks up at me. "Just hold me." I wrap my arms around her and lean down into the side of her neck. Damn she's good. We share a knowing smile and hide our smirks. Four gazes glare into my back. This is more fun than I thought it would be. Lemons and life right?

Dean Whyriss walks onto a makeshift raised earth platform. Professors Heathrow, Julia, Alister and one other I don't know stand behind her.

"Who's the guy on the far right?" I question in Sin's ear.

"That's Professor Locke. He teaches the Knight's elective course for fifth years. He's actually my favorite teacher." She says squeezing my arms with her hands. Professor Locke's orange eyes scan the room before settling on Dean Whyriss.

"I didn't know you wanted to be a knight." I whisper. She would actually be a really good one.

"Of course. I did tell you who my dad was right." She gives me a smile and I nod smiling back.

"Do you know what's going on?" I repeat my earlier question and she shrugs.

"I'm sure we're about to find out."

Dean Whyriss steps up to a microphone and her voice carries out over the sea of students. "Students." She addresses. "Reports have come in from around the realm that Filchers have been spotted." Her voice echoes in the large space. Gasps ring out across the room. "The school was built centuries ago to unite the people and stop this very same evil from taking over the realm. We are once again being called to arms." Silence from all of us.

Filchers are animated corpses that look very lifelike, they run around with incredible speed and strength taking the soul from anything they can get their teeth on. They survive by eating living things. The worst part, if a Filcher eats your soul completely you turn into one of them.

"We've prepared you for the world at the Academy. Now we must prepare you for war." The other professors step forward hand in hand. "My Quint and I will be working closely with the students in the war program. Go now and rest. We won't get much time to do that after tonight."

Sin tilts her head up to me. "You don't think..." She trails off, actually whispering this time.

"Yeah I do." This has the Regent's name all over it. I whip my eCrystal out of my pocket and dial Sir Howin. I have to make sure that he is informed and safe.

"Who are you calling? Your other whores?" Callum sneers at me and I give him a blank look. Sin just smirks at him and rubs my masculine chest.

I look him right in the eye when I speak into the eCrystal. "Sir Howin, did you hear the news?" I question not bothering to greet him as our people do. Callum rolls his eyes and leans against Kyro. The latter hasn't tried to look my way at all since our talk earlier today. Well actually yesterday since it's 0300.

"Yes I've heard the news. What are your orders sir?" Sir Howin picks up on the fact that I'm not alone and uses male pronouns.

"Be careful. Your top priority should be yourself. Souls be safe." My order falls from my tongue. The black sun on my palm warms in approval of the order.

"Souls be safe." He replies back and I hang up.

I lean down and kiss Sin on the cheek. "See you in Extra Lessons?" I question.

"I'll be there." She gives my hand a squeeze then takes off into the throngs of moving bodies. Everybody is leaving except us. Looking around I notice the other Quints aren't moving either.

I send a questioning look to Callum since he usually answer me, but he ignores me. I shrug my shoulders and wait with the others. Once everyone has left except for the Quints and Dean Whyriss's Quint. Everybody moves at once, me a step behind. It's no fun being out of the loop.

"Is this everyone?" Dean Whyriss questions and Professor Julia nods. "Good, let's begin."

Professor Julia kneels down, the concrete beneath us rumbles and start moving. A large circle forms in the middle and then I'm sitting in a concrete chair. Correction. Everyone is sitting in a concrete chair. Professor Julia just made a conference table and sat fifty-five people just like that. Minerals are so cool and creative. They should really be thanking Goddess Totalia more often.

"Time mark is 0327 hours. First Lustrum war meeting may commence." Professor Locke states and an older student to his left starts writing things down.

"I wasn't joking earlier when I said we must now prepare you for war. As Quints training at the Academy, you will be expecting to fight." Dean Whyriss starts eyeing everyone sitting at the table. "Your power levels far outrank that of the other students. There are two major changes that will happen. First, your day will now begin at 0500 with Professor Locke. You will be trained in the art of combat and weapons."

Several of the students starts to protest and the Dean simply holds her hand up and silence fall across the table. "Yes you have your magic but remember. Magic is not without its limits. You may find yourself in a situation where you cannot use your magic or you have used it up." Nods from around the table. "Second, you will be introduce to destruction magic." This time, no one speaks. Destruction magic is no joke. It is extremely dangerous to both the castors and the intended target. Accidents often occur leading to horrible deaths. "Can you now grasp the severity of the situation?" She questions everyone.

"Yes ma'am!" We all roar in unison.

Millions of people are going to die. Guilt tears at my insides. Because of me. My mind unhelpfully adds.

"War meeting end time 0352. Dismissed." Professor Locke barks out and the concrete table and chairs melt back into the ground.

We stalk out of the room and back to the house. I feel like my alarm goes off as soon as my head hits the pillow. It probably actually does.

I quickly shower and put on my combat uniform. I don't think I'll be wearing my regular uniform for a while. I meet the Quint in the kitchen. No one says a word and I stare at my food while everyone else eats. I've refused to eat anything Callum has prepared since he force the potion down my throat.

"Eat." Silas commands. I hate to waste good food but Callum lost my trust and I won't risk it. Even if it means I starve. "You're going to need your strength." Silas tries to reason with me.

"No thanks." I rasp and lean my head against my hand. "I almost died last time." Callum flinches and stares down at his own meal. Good, he should feel bad.

"But you didn't." Silas shoots back at me. "I will not have you passing out from hunger, so either you eat willingly or you will be force fed." He glares at me as if saying 'try me'.

I push away from the table and grab an apple from the center island in the kitchen and take a big bite out of it. I chew with way more force than necessary and make a big show of swallowing. "Happy?"

A vein pops in his forehead. "Very." He snaps. "Let's go." He rises from his seat the other three following suit. I quickly finish my apple because, damn, I really am hungry.

***

After an hour of learning hand-to-hand combat I decide that I hate it and don't understand how the guards could beat me for hours without a break. I'm huffing and puffing after one measly hour.

Of course the the four Princes are barely breaking a sweat. But let's be fair, they didn't spend the last twenty one years in a cage. I think I'm doing pretty good considering. Add in the fact that I almost average five hours of sleep every night and I'm absolutely killing it. Scratch that, I'll only be getting two hours of sleep now. I'm def going to need to find time to nap during the day. Maybe during lunch? No. If I'm not eating good meals at the house for breakfast and dinner then I definitely need to eat a good lunch.

My mind stops rambling when Professor Locke dismisses us and sends us to our core classes. The halls buzz with paranoia.

I fall asleep in our third class and am rudely woken up by an elbow in the ribs by Callum. I guess he doesn't feel as bad as I thought. Dick. It was a really good dream. I was having a nap in my nap. Perfect. I rub my eyes and send Callum my best glare before focusing back on the lesson.

I rush out of the room as quickly as possible and race to the dining hall. I figured that if I eat quickly enough I can head to my next class early and have a nap before the lesson starts. The added bonus is that I get to avoid the Prince's. It's actually brilliant and that's exactly what I do. I figure the best place to nap is in the room of my next class, Plasma. Or that would have been the plan if the door was unlocked, instead I nap in the window seat closest to the classroom and hope that the sound of the other students footsteps wakes me up.

It does, thankfully. I should have set an alarm but my brain was too tired to work. I'll be sure to do that next time. I get through my next two classes without falling asleep by some miracle and head to the west wing for my Quint class.

There's no reason to change since we've all been in our combat uniform since this morning. Thank the Gods that they have some sort of enchantment on them to keep them from smelling bad.

Professor Alister starts the class with a sternness that I didn't know he was capable of. "Form your Quints and we will start the introduction to destruction magic." Everyone breaks away to form the groups and I stand between Silas and Lucian like last time.

"Do you think you'll be able to manage for today?" Professor Julia questions me. "I know you haven't been cleared yet but our circumstances have changed."

I look at the Princes and sigh. "It'll only hurt me if we try."

"That's the spirit." Professor Julia smacks me in the back. It was meant as an encouraging pat but I fight with every muscle in my face to keep my features neutral. Instead of speaking I hold my hands out of Lucian and Silas. They take them without any complaints, and Professor Julia remains close just incase.

The connection snaps into place and my magic wants to leap forward but training with Sinclair and Professor Heathrow helps me control it. I slowly let my magic forward and it connect with Lucian and Silas. I hear them both let out a shaky sigh and look at them both rapidly. They don't appear to hurt so I continue, pushing my magic through them and into Kyro and

Callum. The same thing happens to them. I give them all a questioning glance but none of them answer.

"Give them a minute." Professor Julia comments. "I'm sure they're figuring out what to do with all your power." She gives me a smile.

"Damn." Callum groans, his head falling forward.

"Do I need to pull back?" I question quickly, already trying to bring my magic back to me. Lucian and Silas tighten their hands on mine.

"No." Lucian speaks in his rumble. "There's just a lot to sort through." He grunts through clenched teeth.

I quickly check that my emotions are locked down and give a little sigh of relief when they are. It's my turn to groan when Lucian's magic comes forth. Then Callum's, Kyro's, Silas's. The circle is complete. Sweat drips off my chin and the others fare no better. All of us breath deeply, concentrating on control. Power ripples through the air in tune with our in sync heart beat.

"Very good." Professor Julia circles us. Watching the connection like a hawk. "Maintain." She commands. "Get to know each other's magic."

Mine is first. Plasma sparks through my veins and then theirs, it comes to life in the center of the circle arcing into the air and next the colors of everyone's soul comes into focus. I know the guys see it too when they look around the room. Four eyes land on me after a bit and I shake my head at them, answering an unspoken question. "I cannot see any of your souls. I don't think the bond allows it." They nod. I pull back my magic and Lucian's steps forward.

I can feel the minerals in everything around us, I don't know what any of them are but I'm sure Lucian does. It is his power after all. Shapes form in the center of our circle morphing from one to the next, never truly forming a shape. An awareness flows through me and I can sense all the enchantments in Lucian's braids. The other Prince's eyes follow then they land on the earring in my ear. Our gazes more around the room falling on the other enchantments. Lucian pulls his magic back then Callum's steps forward.

Water pulls from us and flows in a circular waterfall in the center. It roars against itself in it's eternal flow. My awareness falls to the water in all of our bodies. To the blood in my veins and I shiver. Callum just became a little scary. The water changes colors as I feel Callum change it with Alchemy. Feel the changes in property and purpose. Callum pulls his magic back and Kyro's steps forward.

Air whips around the circle and ruffles our hair before coiling tighter in the center making a funnel. I can feel it in my lungs and across my skin as parts of it dance through our senses. "I can't show how my healing works but you are able to feed your magic into me to make it stronger." Kyro explains to me. I guess the other three would already know this. I nod my head and single out Kyro through the connection and then push my magic into him and let go. He gasps and drops his head forward. "Yeah that was right. Maybe not as much next time though." I send a small smile. Kyro pulls his magic back and Silas's steps forward.

Heat brushes across all of our bodies making the sweating worse. The a flame roars to life in the center. It dances in its violent show. Flickering towards all of us in different patterns and combinations. The flames start shaping into different symbols, changing colors as it does. Intentions flow through through everyone. "I also can't really show how my Runes work but this is close. I have to draw them on with my finger but you get the picture. You can also feed your magic into me just like with Kyro." I nod and do the same as I did with Kyro, but I give a little less magic this time. Silas still lets out a little gasp but nods his head and pulls his magic back.

"Very good." Professor Julia claps her hands. "Again. Tomorrow we will work on doing more than one at a time."

We go again, and again. We keep going until class is dismissed.

Chapter 9: Truth is better than Lies.

Lucian Vander Kavalyov

Two days later

I've been following him. Scratch that, I've been stalking him in my spare time. Or I would be but Valdis doesn't go anywhere except school and classes. Not including whatever he did this weekend with Sinclair but Valdis is right. A gentleman shouldn't kiss and tell. He's driving me mad. I also hat that he wears the earring I made for Atlas. Only the people I care about are allowed to wear the things I make. I would have taken it back by now but he never takes it off. He's only been here a week but I've decided he shouldn't have the earring.

A pale hand traces across my darker chest. I pull Callum closer to me in bed, he's been staying here since Atlas preformed the ritual and I can't complain. I love his company even if we are simply cuddling in this moment.

"Good morning." Callum rumbles in my ear and kisses my cheek before slowly, languidly, pulling himself from the bed and walks to the doorframe of my bathroom. "You coming?" He purrs and I damn sure am going to.

Callum turns into the bathroom without waiting form me and I hear the water turn on. Steam quickly starts to escape the bathroom.

Entering I find his naked silhouette behind the glass of my walk-in shower. I strip my boxers from my body and step in behind him grabbing him by the hips and pull his warmed toned body against my chest.

"You're feeling very cheerful this morning." I growl in his ear as my hand travels down the front of his body and grab his hardened cock. Callum lets out a delicious gasp when I start to pump him slowly. His head falls back against my shoulder and he presses his ass against my cock between us.

"More." He moans and I pump him faster, grinding myself agains the crease of his ass cheeks. The hot water falling on us and running down the ridges of our muscles. I press Callum against the dark stone of the shower and trail my hand down his back. Callum arches his back and sends me a flirty wink over his shoulder. "Please." He begs for my touch.

"You beg so pretty for me." I growl and reward him by pumping two fingers into him. It's been a while since we've fucked. Callum's moan is guttural and it lights a fire in my soul. I pump faster then add a third finger. Callum pulls away and spins grabbing the bottle of lube on the shower shelf and grabs my cock firmly.

"Stop teasing me and give me your cock now Lucian." Callum demands, his glowing blue eyes lidded heavily as he lubes my cock up for me. "I need you." He begs and I lose it. I wanted to be gentle for him but I need him just as badly as he needs me. It really has been too long.

My lips slam against his and I lift him, he wraps his legs around my waist and I slam him back against the shower wall. He moans in my mouth when I enter him and I eat his sounds of pleasure. His hands tangle in my braids, keeping my head in place so he can devour me in return and I groan. Callum can't help but try and take control. I smirk in our kiss and slide my hand between our bodies and grasp his cock again. He tries to grab my hand and stop me but I use my magic to morph the wall into shackles and lock his hands against the shower wall. He looks absolute delicious bound like that. At my mercy.

"Stop." Callum moans into my mouth. "I'm gonna cum." I move my hips faster.

"Then cum." I growl out kissing down his neck when he throws his head back. The sounds that fall from his lips when he cums is the most incredible thing I've ever heard. I've missed his sounds of pleasure.

I grunt my pleasure into his throat and pull out, releasing myself onto the shower wall. When I look up Callum is pouting at me. "What?" I search him in concern. "Did I hurt you?" I release my magic holding his wrists and catch him when he falls forward.

"I wanted you to cum inside me." The brat pouts at me. I slowly help him settle his feet on the ground.

"You and I both know that you would complain all day that it keeps dripping out of you." Callum's cheeks flame and he grumbles under his breath but I ignore him and turn him into the spray of the shower. Grabbing the shampoo I wash his hair, giving him a good head scratch. Next is his body and I take extra care of his back and legs, massaging the kinks out of them. Satisfied I go to start washing my braids but Callum stops me and grabs the shampoo from me.

"Let me." I nod at him and he gets to work on my braids. "We're gonna need to rebraid them this weekend." Callum says inspecting my regrowth. I give him another nod. He often helps me braid my hair and I adore him for it. He washes my body for me next then we both get out of the shower. Callum uses his magic to pull the excess water out of my braids then pushes me into the vanity chair. He pulls the oils form my cabinet and oils my scalp. Massaging it into my skin. I relax into his long fingers, a sigh leaving my lips.

"Thank you." I say when he's done and start the long task of putting all the gold enchanted charms into my braids. The task brings me back to the knowledge that Valdis wears one of my creations. He shouldn't.

Callum and I quickly put on our training uniforms and head to the kitchen.

"Do you think he will eat what I make today?" Callum asks while preparing our morning meal. Throwing different herbs and concoctions into it.

"No." I answer simply and his shoulders fall. The anger I have for Valdis is back in full force at upsetting Callum.

"He's getting thinner, have you noticed?" Glowing blue eyes find mine and I see that the thought is actually concerning to Callum. It takes me back a little. "It's okay that he isn't eating what I make, but he needs to eat something."

"Then he can wake up earlier and make his own food." I state simply and start setting the table for the others. Another voice makes me pause.

"He won't." Kyro says. His white hair pulled into a high ponytail. It accentuates his cheek bones nicely. "Valdis barely wakes up in time for combat training." Kyro leans against the doorway, his gold eyes studying me and Callum. "You guys are back together again." He states with a smile and comes over to help me finish setting the table. "Good."

Callum and I look at each other before boxing Kyro between us. His blush lighting up his pale cheeks and making his glowing gold eyes stand out that much more. He looks between us with both desire and confusion. Callum and I lean down at the same time and kiss Kyro on either side of the neck. A small squeak leaves Kyro followed by a low moan.

"I was gonna ask for coffee but I'm wide awake now." Silas purrs from the kitchen entrance.

Callum and I pull away from Kyro with grins. I go back to setting the table and Callum finishes up breakfast. Kyro tries to get his breathing under control and it makes my grin widen on my face.

"Let's eat." Callum cheers and we all take our places at the table.

Valdis doesn't make his way to us until we're heading out the front door.

***

I've been hyper aware of the earring all day. The enchantment has been on all day. He's been abusing the power all day. I'm pissed. I'm fucking fuming. He never should have had the enchantment in the first place. What the hell does a pampered Prince like him need an enchantment for pain management for anyway. He doesn't deserve it.

The bastard doesn't even come home after his classes anymore. I know he doesn't want to be part of our Quint but he is and Valdis needs to fucking deal with it instead of spending every moment he can in the fucking library.

That being said, why the hell is the enchantment running while he's sitting in the damn library. He's not doing a damn thing besides flipping pages and typing on his eTop.

I've had it. He never should have had it in the first place.

My senses expand and my focus stops on my enchantment in Valdis's ear. It's my enchantment so it listens to my will, this task would be much harder for any other Mineralist to do but for me it's as easy as breathing. I crack the white stone in the gold earring breaking the enchantment. I know I fucked up as soon as it happens.

Valdis's posture turns to stone. He becomes absolutely rigid in his seat. A small gasp is the only thing he lets out. Then he closes the book in front of him with slow motions. Packs away his eTop into his back and stands from his seat. He walks stiffly out the back door.

I race after him, pulling my eCrystal from my pocket and calling the first name that pops up. They answer on the first ring. "I fucked up, get here now." I yell into the phone trailing Valdis into the woods behind the library.

Chapter 10: Lies are better than the Truth.

Valdis Spyridon Aritiri

Present

I have no idea where I'm going. I just need to get away from prying eyes. I need to fall apart by myself. The pain is so intense. I didn't realize how much the enchantment took the pain away until right now. In this moment I understand how much the enchantment helped. I heard a crack then felt all of it again.

How did I survive this for so long with nothing but myself?

My shoulder hits a tree shooting more pain through my body. I grab onto the trunk for support then double over and hurl my guts up. Silent sobs leave my throat and my breath won't stop heaving. In. Out. In. Out. I'm breathing way too quickly. Bending over hurts more so I pull myself upright. The scent of my own bile is making me more nauseous. I take no more than four steps forward before my knees hit the earth.

Something is wrong. My back never hurt this badly.

Sweat covers my body but my limbs are chilled. Shock? My breathing keeps heaving in and out of my body and my vision swims. Anger fills my body and I rip the earring from my ear. I go to throw it but stop short and tuck it into one of my many pockets instead. Real sobs finally break from my lips. My forehead hits the ground.

"I'm sorry Atlas." I choke out through my ruined throat. A cough wracks my entire body sending more pain through me. I can feel the flesh tear on my back and a silent scream leaves me. My magic runs through my body but refuses to leave me and I wonder why until a voice sends me flinching.

"Valdis, what the fuck?" Lucian comes into view his glowing green eyes tracking the tears on my face to the position I'm in. Prone if you're wondering.

"I'm fine, go away." I whisper out, turning my face into the dirt and gritting my teeth. My stomach rolls and I dry heave into the ground.

"Not a chance pretty boy." Silas calls from my other side. I'm too tired to look at him. "Let's go." I'm assuming he's talking to Lucian because if not fuck him.

A broken scream rips from my lips when Silas and Lucian lift me off the ground from under my shoulders. My legs too weak to hold me. We start heading in some directions that I'm in too much pain to deal with. I have no idea where they're taking me.

"We're almost at the house, be ready." Silas talks into his eCrystal. "Lucian said something about his enchantment breaking." Silas pauses but their sprint doesn't. "I see the house." He hangs up and they both almost break the door down in their rush. I'd be touched but I'm trying to stay conscious.

Kyro and Callum are both standing in the living room. Callum has potions flooding his arms and Kyro's hands are glowing gold reaching for me. "No."

I try to shout but can't manage the energy for it. I try to pull from Silas and Lucian but it's no use. Kyro places his hands on my waist and I melt. I melt into his chest burying my face into his neck. The pain goes away. All of it. We slowly sink to our knees. I've never felt this good in my entire life. Not that I can remember. A groan leaves my lips. Bliss.

Something wet hits my shoulder and I pull back slightly to see what. Kyro's face comes into view and he's... He's crying. Why is he crying? I tilt my head in confusion and reach my hand out to wipe his tears then pause before I touch him. I can't touch him. A frown forms on my face. Then it clicks. HE'S TOUCHING ME!

I fling myself away from him falling backwards onto my ass and elbows. Kyro's breathing like he just did our combat training workout five times without stopping. The pain is back and I grit my teeth, a different groan leaving.

"I told you not to touch me." I heave out. Kyro's head flings up and he glares at me.

"Have you just been walking around with that much pain since you got here? What the hell was that Valdis?" Kyro shouts at me, crawling to his feet and stalks towards me. He's pissed.

"It's none of your damn business." I growl out and try to stand but fall. A gasp leaves my lips and I start sweating again. Kyro pauses his glowing gold gaze concerned. "I don't want your pity." I grab the side of the cough and pull myself to my feet.

"It is my Gods damned business when a member of my Quint is in so much pain that he can barely stand. When his pain brought me to my fucking knees." Kyro shouts and to prove his point I sway and Callum has to grab me before I hit the ground. "What the fuck is going on? That isn't normal pain Valdis."

"Front right pocket." Lucian commands bringing my attention to him instead of Callum and Kyro. I'm quickly brought back to reality when Callum's hand fishes into my pocket, dangerously close to my nonexistent dick. He pulls the earring from my pocket and quirks up and eyebrow.

"Hey!?" I shout and try to grab it from him but only manage a step before I hit the ground again. My vision swimming and stomach dry heaving. "That's mine." I gasp out. "It was a gift from Atlas." My voice breaks on his name. "Give it back." I don't care how they see me anymore but they can never know. Lies are better than the truth. "I have a chronic illness." The lie falls from my lips. "Atlas knew, it's why he gave me the enchantment." I look up at Kyro's stricken face. "It can't be healed."

"That's why..." Kyro trails off. A green flash brings my gaze to Lucian and he's walking towards me. He won't look at me when he slides the earring back into my ear. He doesn't look at me when I finally catch my breath. And not when I start speaking again.

"I didn't need the reminder." I pull myself up and dust my pants off. The enchantment is noticeably stronger than last time.

"It'll need to be recharged once a week." Lucian whispers. "I'm sorry. I didn't know." When I turn my questioning eyes on him he continues. "I thought you took it from Atlas so I broke the enchantment on it. I made it for him."

A sigh leaves my lips and I turn my back on them. "It's okay. I didn't want anyone to know." My shoulders sag. "If we're done here, I'm going to bed."

"We are definitely not done here." A voice clips out. Of course it's Silas. Instead of getting pissed at him I decide I don't have the energy. Instead I turn back to the couch and sink into it. Silas sits across from me into the other couch and the other Princes sink into the remaining seats. "More details." Silas commands.

"I was diagnosed three years ago." Follow as closely to the truth as possible. "I've been to healers all over the realm." Total lie. Silas's eye twitches. "Atlas didn't know all of it just that I was in pain and it had gotten worse over the years." Truth.

"Will it kill you?" Kyro interrupts and all eyes shoot to him. "You said it was getting worse." He looks down into his lap.

"Yes." I say simply. All eyes shoot to me now. "There have only been two other cases of this illness in the realm. They both died within three months of their diagnosis." Basically the truth of the Iron Coffin.

"You said you've been diagnosed for three years though?" Callum questions, his head tilting like he's solving the world's hardest math problem.

"That is true. I'm currently the longest survivior. No one knows when I'm going to die, just that it will kill me." I smile softly. "It could be any second or in a century." I look down at my hands. "I don't think Atlas knew that much or else he probably wouldn't have preformed the ritual." Silence greets me.

"Probably not." Lucian agrees. "Or he figured it out and that's why he did it. He was the best of us." Nods follow his statement.

"If we're done I'm going to bed." I glance at the clock and see that I have thirty minuets before my hour of fun.

"We're done for now." Silas, the proper ass, says dismissing me with a wave.

I make it into my room then out my window and through the woods.

How much more of this can I take?

***

"Did you hear?" Sinclair grabs my arm in the hallway between classes. The four Princes have been practically attached to my hip since last night. "They're sending fifth years and the Quinta on missions."

I grab her arm and pull her into a less crowded part of the hallway pressing her back against a wall and placing my arm above her head leaning close. "What do you mean missions?"

"Apparently people are going missing all over the realm. The kingdoms don't want to cause panic so they're sending us on recon missions. Not to engage unless necessary. All findings must be reported to the council." She leans in closer and whispers directly into my ear. "Regent Lukadious is on the council." She leans back giving me a meaningful look. I nod at her.

"When will the announcement be made?" Silas interrupts our moment.

"During Lunch." She looks to my mouth then back at me. I see her question before she even expresses it and give a small nod. She presses her lips to mine in a quick kiss. "See you at the next war meeting." And then she's gone.

I press my fingers to my lips. I know I nodded at her but that was like my first actual kiss. At least one that I was okay with happening. All the companion workers they hired for the tabloid photos were kind but I didn't have a choice in the matter. Sinclair was my first real kiss. Yes it was a peck but still. It totally counts.

A voice clears and I look at Callum. "Are we going to class or just standing around all day?" He looks pissed. I have to tell Sin all about this, she's gonna laugh so hard.

We all move to our next class waiting for lunch to arrive.

Just as Sin said. The announcement happens at lunch then the War cariculum moves into the West wing.

***

"Professor?" I call out to Professor Julia. "Are you sure I'm ready to go out on missions?" She and I both know that I am not prepared to use magic in an actual perilous situation.

"For recon only missions I believe you are ready." She smacks my back and I bite down a wince. Lucians new enchantment is great but it's a little slow to react. I think because it's stronger it's slower to get started on new pains.

I give her a small nod and head off with the other Prince's to grab my go bag and load up on the giant EMC. The Academy is keeping the "Royal Quint" closer to the Academy and the Prince's have noticed. I'm honestly okay with it. Less chance that Regent Lukadious can find me.

"Are they keeping us close because we're royal or is it because the Lazy Prince is with us?" Silas asks loudly to the poor fifth year driving us to our destination. Silas does remember that I have a "chronic illness" and he's sill being rude. Dick. "We have the strongest Quint."

"All third years or younger are being kept on the Lustrum continent." The fifth year tells Silas. "I, a fifth year, am with you because you are royal." He adds unhelpfully.

Silas shoot a glare at me as if that is at all my fault. I send him snooty look back and he scoffs and looks out the window.

"Just because we're sticking close to the Academy doesn't mean that our mission is any less important." Kyro chimes in and Silas nod at him then himself. As though he's confirming with himself that this is important. "What's our objective?" Kyro asks the fifth year.

"We're investigating the disappearance of a young woman named Zoa. We are to determine if she left on her own or was taken." He states simply, his orange eyes tracking all of us through the mirror. "Get some rest while you can. It's going to be a long drive."

We all do as he says, or at least I do. I wake with my head on Callum's shoulder and I have to say that I'm slow to pull away. Callum may not have intended for it to give me some sense of comfort but the contact was nice. Lucian catches my gaze before I can pull away and he sends me a soft smile. Weird. I turn away from them before I can catch any other expressions from any of them. "Are we here?" I ask as I see us pulling through the back of a town and heading out into the woods. The sun is just setting over the mountains in the horizon.

"Almost." The fifth year says. "Guards up. All the information given is that Zoa lives on the outskirts of her small town. She was reported missing three days ago by her coworkers at the local veterinary clinic." He says as we pull into the woman's front drive. Her house is dark with no lights on anywhere. The fifth year slinks out of the EMC and we all follow suit forming into a triangle with him at the front and me finding myself in the second row with Lucian.

Fifth year.

Lucian, me.

Silas, Kyro, Callum.

Apparently this formation is the strongest since we are able to form a Quint as quickly as possible. But I find it strange since Lucian can neutralize my powers where as Kyro or Callum could strengthen them. Or I could strengthen Silas?

We get to the front door and the fifth year knocks silently. We all stay quiet while we wait for a response but silence is our only greeting. He knocks again and nothing happens. Lucian squeezes his large frame in beside the fifth year and places his hand around the doorknob his eyes start to glow more brightly and his hands follow suit. He's manipulating the minerals in the door to unlock it.

Also, we would apparently be really bad at playing 'hide and go seek in the dark'. Our eyes are like damn glow sticks out here.

A 'snick' sounds and the door slowly creaks open on screaming hinges. Chills run up and down my metal spine and an eerie feeling floods my senses.

Something is wrong.

The tenseness I see in the others lets me know that they can feel it too. We slowly file into the dark house and Lucian grabs my hand. I look at him in questioning and feel his magic probe mine. He uses his other hand to point at my eyes and I nod. He wants me to look for souls. I focus my magic and feel the magic glow more intensely in my eyes as I look around. All I can see is the small orange and white color of the fifth year's soul. A nice soul.

"I can't see any other soul besides-" I gesture towards him and he lets out a small chuckle.

"Guess I didn't introduce myself, names Raymond, just call me Ray." He gives a small grin and stands up straight. "Neat trick, I didn't know third years could do that." He scratches his shaved head.

"I'm kinda a special case." I mutter under my breath and Silas scoffs.

"No matter. Check the rooms in teams of two. Prince Valdis, you're with me. Prince Kyro and Silas are a team. Prince Lucian and Callum are a team." He eyes everyone waiting for any adverse reaction, I can sense Silas biting his tongue. "Report all findings to me. K&S you're upstairs, L&C will be in the basement, and V and I will be on the ground floor. Dismissed." The other four break off, Ray and I start our search from the front door and don't find anything until we get to the mud room at the back.

Claw marks run up and down the walls on all sides and the back door is in splinters. I squat down and inspect it while Ray inspects the claw marks.

"Looks like it was broken in from the outside." I muse to him and he grunts in response. My gaze falls down to the wooden floorboards and note the scratches lead out into the woods, the blood is still wet. The sun finishes setting and it gives the forest a dark sinister look. I of course, start to follow the tracks into the woods. The light from the stars and two moons all I have to see by, it's normally enough but tonight feels darker.

My steps are slow and I'm all too aware that Ray hasn't followed me outside when I find myself deep in the forest and go to ask him if we should turn back. He isn't there and that cements my decision to leave the creepy af forest post haste.

"Did... YooOOOuuuu... Commme... For... MeeeEEEeee?" Forget chills my metal spine just got frost bite. The voice sounds like two people talking at the same time. A woman's voice layered with a man who sounds like he's been smoking the bad stuff. I wish my fight or flight response choose freeze instead but no. I turn slowly and come face to face with a Flicker. A gasp lodges in my throat. It looks almost human and that's the worst part. The Flicker stumbles closer into my view on boney legs. "PllleeassSSee. .. saaYYyy... YouuUUU... caaammeee... forrrr... MMMeeee." The Flicker says and reaches for me. It's lifeless eyes roll into the back of it's head and then it's mouth splits apart revealing rows and rows of razor sharp teeth. No wonder it had trouble speaking.

My body flings back and Plasma sparks to life across my shoulders. I silently thank Ray for not noticing I left because now I don't have to hold back. My Plasma sparks into the air and lights up the forest around us and oh fuck.

I'm gonna die.

We are not alone. There has to be at least nine other Flickers moving to surround me. One of them has fresh blood coating their fingers and realize that they are intelligent enough to set a trap, and I'm dumb enough to fall for it.

Claws tear into my left arm, and then all hell breaks loose.

Chapter 11: Magic go Zappy Zap

The attacks come from all sides at the same time and my Plasma pulses out of me in a wave sending all the Flickers flying away from me. The scent of burning flesh and ozone fills the air. They recover, which I didn't expect at all. The voltage I used would have killed a horse and here they are jumping back onto feet that are no longer pretending to be weak. One launches at me and I dodge, barely. Thank you Professor Locke. The next one hits me square in the chest and I fly back through the air hitting a tree. Plasma arcs from my core and zaps the bastard away from me. Another one jumps at me and I slide to the left sending the Flickers body crashing through the tree. The trees falls to the earth with a loud 'boom' and I get to my feet quickly. Holy shit. How strong are they?

I try to lead them towards Zoa's house back to my Quint but I can't, they're already leading me further into the woods. Not allowing me to take a single step towards the house.

A stabbing pain shoots through my left calf and a broken scream roars from my throat. A Flicker is biting me, I can feel my soul start to pull from my body and the panic finally gets to me. I'm in actual danger here. I grab the foul creature by it's face and pour my Plasma, amping it up to the highest voltage I can. It shrieks then explodes. Blood and guts fall off my shoulders and face, sparks lighting up all over my body and a shake flows through my limbs.

"That was disgusting." I say as I pull the Flicker's skin off my face. I don't have time to recover before I'm slammed into the ground by my face, my nose crunches on the impact but I don't have time to focus on it when razor sharp teeth are digging into my right shoulder. My Plasma shoots out of me at the same voltage as before and another Flicker explodes.

Good magic.

I don't get more than my knees under me before I'm being kicked in the side, my ribs shatter on impact, and I fly through the air coming to an abrupt stop against another tree. The air is knocked out of me and my lungs scream for oxygen, blood seeping from my mouth. Breathing isn't an option when two Flickers come at me at the same time. Teeth sinking into my forearm the other bites my shin. Their strong jaws grind my bones against one another. My magic is slower to respond this time and I have to force it through my veins. They both let out a horrible shriek then I'm showered in their matter. I spit flesh from my open mouth, the coppery taste disgusting and finally suck some oxygen into my lungs.

Where the fuck is everyone?

I'm blindsided by another Flicker when it punches me in the jaw. My vision goes dark but I refuse to black out. I refuse to die here. The Regent tried to shred my soul and failed. His guards tried to destroy my body and failed. These damn creatures will not succeed where he failed. They won't. They can't.

Teeth sink into my side and my magic flares again. The Flicker explodes. I'm starting to get a little cold form all this... liquid... on me.

How many Flickers was that? Five?

A foot presses down on my wrist and a crunch sounds. I'm grabbed by my black and white curls and pulled up from the ground. Teeth sink into my throat and another sink into my thigh and left hand. I can feel my soul being sucked from me more forcefully. My magic sparks at an even slower pace, another set of teeth bite into my lower back and my magic all but putters out.

I'm going to die.

My eyes slowly fall closed. My body giving up the fight. No. NO! My magic roars to life again and four 'pops' sound in the night. I crash to my knees holding myself up with my good arm and heave breath in and out of my lungs. My eyes slowly look around me searching for the last Flicker and I see it running into the woods. Escaping. Not on my watch. My magic arcs from my hand and slams into the Flicker, it explodes on impact. No loose ends.

I'm slow to recover and sway on my feet when I use a tree to prop myself up. My vision swims and refocuses on the bitemarks all over my body that are seeping blood into the earth. If the Flickers aren't going to kill me then the bleeding will. I look around and can't decide which way to go.

Tug.

The fucking bond.

My body starts walking in the direction of the others, the bond pulling me in the right direction. I thought it would have gone away after a while but apparently if I don't know where to go it'll tell me. My pace is slow. I'm pretty sure a snail moves faster then I do at this moment. Each step agony. All I want to do is lay down and go to sleep but that isn't an option. Not until I can get myself somewhere safe, and as much as I hate it, safe just so happens to be with my Quint. The same Quint who never showed up during my fight. "Be your own hero." I snark to myself.

I hear the Princes and Ray well before I see them, but I'm much too tired to call out to them.

"Where the fuck is he Raymond?" Silas sounds absolutely pissed. I can see the glow of his orange magic through the trees. He's gripping Ray, with flaming hands, by the collar.

"I don't know. We were investigating the back room and then he was gone. I shouted for you as soon as I noticed but who knows how long that took me. Prince Valdis is a quiet person." Ray says quickly. I guess he's right? I don't really talk that much? I didn't tell him I was leaving.

"Silas," Kyro interrupts. "This isn't helping. We need to go look for him."

"We wouldn't have to look if the brat would leave his side of the bond open." Lucian grumbles and Callum nods. Dicks.

I've decided to walk into the clearing with the confidences of a thousand men. Me, injured, absurd. I take my first step into the clearing and I, of course, trip and fall. I gasp and my legs choose this moment to give out. "Fuck." Traitors. I catch my fall with my good wrist and decide that the ground isn't so bad. I think I'm just gonna stay here. I don't think anyone noticed that anyway. Is that a leaf? What a pretty leaf. It's got all the colors, orange, yellow, red, and even some green. Gods I'm tired.

"The hell do you think you're doing, Lazy Prince? You can't just wonder off whenever you feel like it." Silas says in his ever pompass way. "Get off the floor, we have a job to do."

I can't muster the energy to respond to him, instead my good arm gives out and I collapse. I'm grabbed by the waist and flipped around. I let out another gasp, this time in pain. My vision swims during the motion and when they decide to focus again, I'm staring up into glowing blue eyes and short wavy gold hair. Golden Prince. Callum's eyes widen when he gets a good look at me.

"Are those teeth marks?!" He shouts at me trailing his fingers across the bite on my throat. "Why are you covered in blood?!"

I'm grabbed away from Callum at lightning speed. Ray is cataloging ever mark he can see, his body tenses going on high alert. His orange eyes flaring with a blinging glow. "Where is it?" He commands. He knows exactly what these bites are from. His orange gaze searches the forest around us.

"They're dead." I use his grip on me to steady myself as I stand back up.

"They?" Raymond asks helping me stay steady as we head back to Zoa's house. He wraps my good arm over his shoulders noting how I keep my other arm tight to my chest. Kyro steps up to my other side and holds his hand out to me hesitantly, asking. I give him a slight nod and he supports my other side. His magic flows into me slowly, focusing on my recent injuries. I'll have to thank him later for not snooping.

"Ten Flickers, about a mile west of here." I grunt when the bones in my wrist pop back into place. "I can lead you there after I regroup."

Ray nods his head and follows Callum through the back door. Kyro breaks away from us when we get into the living room and then he grabs my arm and pulls me down beside him, tucking me into his side.

"Don't make it weird Valdis. The more contact I have with you, the easier it is to heal. Skin to skin is preferred though." I go to shake my head at him but Kyro shushes me. "Stop distracting me. I'm trying to focus on the freshest injuries."

Callum rounds the corner from the kitchen and holds out a glass to me. I'm still too tired to argue and I take the cup gratefully. A delicious numbness flows through my body and I can feel some of my energy coming back. I turn questioning purple eyes on Callum.

"I put some herbs in there to help with the pain and a little more for energy." Callum nods at me and runs his hands together in a nervous gesture. "I hope that's okay?"

"I don't know why you all are fussing. He walked here on his own so he's fine. The Lazy Prince probably lied and there was only one and he got his ass handed to him." Silas sneers. I guess he can't stand that his Quint members are being nice people.

"He had four shattered ribs, a punctured lung, broken nose, broken jaw, broken wrist, nine bites, a concussion, severe blood loss and a bruised spine. Valdis should have died thirty minutes ago." Kyro's voice is cold but I can't focus on that. He spoke about my spine. My head whips to him and I can't breath. He said he would only focus on the recent injuries, not pry into old ones. I guess the Iron Coffin is technically always a recent injury but still. Kyro's glowing gold eyes stare right at me his head tilting to the side, white hair pooling over his shoulder. "We can talk about your recklessness later. How are you feeling right now?" Maybe he doesn't know?

I take stock of my body before I answer. "Pretty good considering." I stand slowly and take a couple steps. Some of the flesh from the Flickers falls from my head and sends a full body shiver through me. "Disgusting." I look down at my body again in the light and a gag makes it's way up my throat. My combat uniform is drenched in blood and guts. "Disgusting." I run a hand through my white and black curls only to find that they're matted with more blood and guts. "Disgus-"

A flood of cold water soaks me to the bone from above. I sputter out then turn towards Callum whose wearing a smirk. "No need to thank me." He laughs.

"It's cold." I say in shock.

"Well yeah." He shrugs and looks away. "I didn't have time to heat it up."

A gust of wind doesn't exactly dry me but I'm no longer a drowned rat. I spin towards Kyro. "You can take a shower later."

"If everyone is done messing around, can we go?" Ray says and pushes away from the wall and starts heading towards the door. We all follow after him. "Prince Valdis, lead the way." He commands and I fall back into good little solider mode and retrace all my steps. It helps that I left bloody finger prints and smears on the trees that I used for support on the way. Everyone is silent as they watch me, as they see how much I struggled getting back.

I stop dead in my tracks when we reach the area where I had my battle. Where I got my ass beat. Red coats almost the entire scene. Raymond walks around me and assess the different piles of burnt flesh. The scent still strong in the air. Silas inspect the felled tree. Kyro is looking at the spot where I had my throat torn into. Callum is staring some guts that made it into a tree. Lucian is standing next to me.

"Why didn't you call for help?" Lucian asks staring at the carnage.

"As if any of you would have heard." I scoff and turn away from the scene, away from them. "As if you would have believed my cries for help."

"I meant through the bond brat." Lucian growls down at me. I stare at him and wait for him to figure it out himself. He takes a step back in shock his braids 'clinking' in the motion. "You didn't think we would have come." It's not a question and we both know it so I ask a question of my own.

"When does the spare ever get saved?" My raspy voice comes out hard and accusing.

"Who hurt you?" Lucian looks at me like he can actually see me. I know he only sees what he wants.

I go to respond to him but my magic flares, my eyes glowing more intensely and awareness floods my body. I ignore Lucian and turn back towards the gruesome scene. Ten cold glowing pink souls float above the mangled corpses of the Flickers, my body move towards them on auto pilot. Pink cords flow from them into my hand and tug one slightly in confusion. I thought flickers didn't have souls? I gently pull the one and the pink peels away leaving behind a bright blue soul. I know without a doubt that it's Zoa's soul. Tears flow down my cheeks. I pull the next soul. Purple. Pull. White. Pull. Green. Pull. Orange. Pull. Grey. Pull. Yellow. Pull. Red. Pull. Navy. Pull. Lilac. Pull. Brown. These uncovered souls feel distressed and scared.

A presence unlike any I've ever felt in my life emerges from behind me. I can feel it ghosting across my body and my own soul, greeting me. "Well done, Reaper of mine." A woman's voice whispers in my ear from behind. "Guide the lost to me so that I may welcome them home." She instructs and I turn. Goddess Valdrestaria is here though I am unable to see her, but I can feel her. My soul greets her gladly. I gather the chords in one hand then kneel before her holding them out. The Goddess takes them and I feel her presence fade away. When I look back the souls are gone too.

"Valdis. What the hell was that?" Silas is pulling me to my feet as if he'd been trying to get my attention for a while. I pay him no mind. I have to find a way to collect all the scattered body parts and give them a proper send off.

"Burn it." Is all I say.

"What?" Silas looks taken aback.

"I said burn it. They may have been monsters in death but they were real people first. They deserve a proper send off." I stare at the mangled corpses.

"This is evidence, we can't just burn it." Lucian argues.

"Then take some pictures! They will receive the Soul Send. I will preform the rest of my duties as Prince of the Kingdom of Souls and as a Reaper. Do not get in my way." I growl at everyone. Plasma sparks across my entire body humming violence at anyone who dares to interfere. I am met with nods and them Silas does as I ask. He burns the entire area where the fight took place. I place my fists together and preform the Soul Send. "May you have peace in the hands of Goddess Valdrestaria, keeper of souls and decider of death. May your journey be safe and good. May you find rest. Souls be safe." My magic calms itself once I have finished and we head back to Zoa's house.

"What was that back there?" Kyro asks bumping my shoulder on the way into the living room of Zoa's. "You were using your Quintessence and kneeling and generally just acting stranger than normal."

I let out a deep sigh and make myself comfortable. Ray hasn't come in yet. Kyro does the same as well as the other three Princes, they were obviously eavesdropping. "I can't tell you much, but Reapers are able to guide souls to Goddess Valdrestaria. I don't really understand it myself and I plan to ask Professor Heathrow as soon as possible." I shrug my shoulders at them.

"Look alive people. The Academy wants us back asap so get your sorry buts in the EMC." Ray commands as he walks into the living room clapping his hands.

"I thought we were going to be staying here for the night?" My question falls from my lips as I stand and grab my bag quickly. What time is it? 19:24. Is that enough time to get back before 00:00?

"This blows, well be getting back at 23:40. Are we at least getting classes off tomorrow?" Callum, ever helpful, groans as he walks out the front door.

Ray doesn't answer Callum about classes. "You will be debriefed at 05:00 in the war room. Don't be late." Ray loads into the EMC and we follow suit. "Get some rest on the ride, Gods know you'll need it."

The four Princes do just that but my eyes never leave the crystal clock, counting down the minutes till my soul is shredded.

Chapter 12: Nobody Likes a Spy

V aldis Spyridon Aritiri

Present, Thursday Night

The clock ticks closer to my demise reading 23:37. The school grounds are nowhere in sight. What the hell is taking so long?

"Ray?" I whisper to him in the drivers seat of the EMC. "Are we almost there?" The princes are all sound asleep and I don't want to risk waking them.

"Should be there in the next fifteen minutes." He whispers back to me picking up on me not wanting to wake the others.

That's cutting it way too close. The crystal clock reads 23:41. "I think I'll get out here. My girlfriend wants to see me before she goes to sleep." Thank you Sin for agreeing to this charade.

"If you're sure." Ray says as he pulls over looking into the trees on either side of the road. I manage to slip past Callum and open the door but when I go to step out a hand snags my arm.

"Where do you think you're going?" Callum grumbles in a sleepy voice waking Kyro in the seat behind him. Glowing golden and blue eyes stare at me.

"Sin wants to see me, and rather than making Ray drive us all over the place like some chauffeur, I decided to get out here and walk." Ray grumbles his thanks and I pull away from Callum give a slight wink then shut the door before they can say anything else. Golden eyes never leaving my face. The EMC takes off and I let out a sigh of relief. That worked better than I thought it would.

I step into the woods quickly and get as far away from the road as possible. I'll need to find a new sanctuary for tonight and quickly since my normal one is on the other side of the campus. I won't be sleeping tonight if I plan to get back in time for the debrief in the morning. I haven't been able to sleep much at all lately. The earring is doing wonders for that but the signs are starting to become more evident.

I find a place. It isn't as far away from the road as I would like but it's enough. For tonight it'll have to be. It's a small clearing in the woods, the trees pushed back far enough that I wont have to worry about them catching on fire when my Plasma sparks to life. I don't have long to prepare. I'm about to remove my tactical belt from my combat uniform when a twig snaps in the brush around me. Plasma sparks across my shoulders and light the area around me up.

"Who's there?" My voice, raspy with damage, comes out cold. The coldest my voice has ever sounded in my life. My Plasma hits the area close to where I heard the twig snap, just out of my range, and a gasp sounds from the tree close to it.

"Cool your jets Valdis." Callum's voice sounds from behind me and I spin around looking from him to the tree I just shot at. My eyes wide with panic go back and forth from Callum to the tree. I know someone is there.

"We just wanted to see what you were up to?" Kyro says and stalks from behind the tree, walking over to Callum and leans against him.

"You've been acting Shady since you got here and we're getting to the bottom of this tonight." Silas says as he comes form behind another tree. I can't sense any of them while I keep the bond closed.

"Are all of you here? Stalking me?" I hiss out at them unable to contain my emotions. I'm panicking and it's coming out as anger. Lucian answers my question by coming out of the woods and standing behind Callum and Kyro. He arches his eyebrow at me as if I'm the one who has explaining to do. I look at my watch and it reads 23:56. Fuck. "You all need to leave right now. My business is mine and no one else's." I keep spinning in frantic circles to look at all four of them. "Please, I promise we can talk about everything but you all need to go. Now."

"We're going to talk about everything now." Silas says shoving me in the chest and I fall back against Callum and Kyro. I glance down at my watch and my shoulders sag in defeat. 23:58. I don't know what I expected them to be able to do in four minutes but it doesn't matter.

"I need all of you to get out of my range, now." My tone serious. I stare at the ground refusing to meet any of their eyes. There's nothing to be done, they're going to see.

"No. We are going to have this conversa-" Silas starts but I cut him off.

"If you don't get out of my range in one minute, you all will die." I remove my tactical belt and fold it in half before holding it up to my mouth. "Do not step within my range until I tell you to do so." My gaze still remains downcast. "The bond is the only reason why I haven't killed any of you already. I will not be in control of myself or my magic. Move. Now." I'm not sure what part of my amazing speech got through to the four of them but they do as I ask and I place the belt between my teeth. What I wouldn't give for a silencing crystal right now. I know they stan in front of me but I refuse to let them see my agony. I turn my back to them.

The pain begins. It feels like fire and knives are gouging through my entire nervous system. I want so badly to stand through this. To not show a single weakness to the Princes behind me. But I can't. The pain is too great and I am too weak. My legs give out and I crash into the earth beneath me. My back twisting and turning, tearing sounds coming from the uniform shirt.

A sob escapes through the belt and I press my face into the dirt and grass to keep anymore from leaving me. My soul screams in the night and I scream right along with it when the pain intensifies. The earth muffles the sounds of my despair. Regent Lukadious must be pissed because I haven't been found yet and he's increased the level of pain inflicted by the Iron Coffin.

My magic sparks around me in a violent halo pulsing with each flare of pain. The hum drowns out my screams and sobs. All of my muscles fighting against something only my soul can feel. My watch chimes and I know it been fifteen minutes. The level of pain continues to rise until I can focus on nothing but forcing my lungs to take my next breath. On surviving. And then it hits me. Do I even want to survive? I let the darkness seep into my vision. Let myself succumb to the pain. Let myself go. Drift into nothingness. I'm dying. Finally. After three years it's finally happening.

The pain stops with a jarring halt. My head rolls to the side out of the dirt and my eyes fall on my watch. The crystal clock face reads 01:00. The session is over. I slowly pull myself to my knees and feel the breeze cool the fresh blood running down my metal spine. My head tilts back to look at the night sky and I scream in an even raspier voice than normal. My earring heating against my skin.

"Why won't you just kill me already!? Coward!" My fists clench and rip the grass from the earth around me and I realize that I am also a coward.

Footsteps sound from behind me then Kyro is sliding on his knees before me. His hands, glowing with golden magic, reach out and pull me into his chest. His breathing is absolutely ragged and I sag into him burying my face. Kyro snakes his hands around my back and places his hands on my bare spine, my hands stay limp at my sides. His healing feels nice on the fresh tears in my back but it does nothing for the pain in my soul. It never will. "Why didn't you tell us?" Kyro whispers and I realize that the other three are surrounding us.

I sigh but don't pull my face away from his chest. I honestly want the comfort and he smells really nice. "There is nothing to tell." I do push away from Kyro now and unsteadily get to my feet. Part of me wishes he didn't heal the skin on my back, it'll just tear again. My eyes find Silas's burning orange ones, his expression looks severe but it always does when it comes to me. "Can we talk about whatever we needed to talk about later? It's been a long day and we need to start walking if we're going to make the debrief." I start to shuffle forward but a hand wraps around mine. The contact is weird enough for me that I look down at the hand then follow the arm all the way up to glowing green eyes.

"Are you okay?" Lucian tilts his head to the side. The enchanted charms in his hair clinking together. I pull my hand from his and turn away.

"We're going to be late." Is all I say and continue walking. We walk in complete silene and I can feel four sets of eyes on my bare spine the whole way back.

Silas decides that we have enough time to stop by the house and get cleaned up before the debrief. It would look weird if we showed up to the meeting covered without looking our best. Well, without wearing a clean combat uniform since classes are scheduled to continue as normal. I'm sure he's just saying that for my benefit. I throw a black hoodie over my combat uniform and meet the others in the foyer. The weather has been steadily been getting colder. Callum has breakfast burritos that he passes out and I take mine with a sigh. I need the energy after yesterday.

We pass our Combat & Weapons class, Professor Locke is notably absent. Our stride doesn't stop until we stand in front of the administration building. Ray stands outside waiting for us. "Glad you could make it." He greets. "Follow me." Ray leads us through the many hallways until we pass by Dean Whyriss's door and go the the one immediately after it. He knocks once then opens the door.

Dean Whyriss, Professor Heathrow, Professor Julia, Professor Alister, and Professor Locke and a fifth year all sit on one side of a long table. The six of us take our seats opposite them.

"Debrief start time, 05:01." Professor Locke calls out and the student starts typing away on an eTop. "Raymond, begin."

"We arrived at Zoa's house at approximately 15:37..." Ray recounts every detail of the trip. "Prince Valdis disappeared around 16:21 then reappeared at 18:37 covered in wounds inflicted by Flickers. After Prince Kyro and Prince Callum healed him, Prince Valdis took us to the location of his attack where I confirmed Zoa was among the bodies of ten Flickers before they were given a Flame Burial at Prince Valdis's request. We left Zoa's house at 19:24 and arrived here before 00:00." All the professors nod their heads at Raymond.

Callum has to poke me in my side during Ray's recounting of the event more than once and I can feel concerned looks from Kyro and Lucian. I ignore all of it. Even one of Callum's pokes which turns into a pinch.

"Prince Valdis, please tell us what prompted you to walk out into the wood without backup?" Professor Locke gives me a disapproving scowl.

A sigh leaves my lips because I know how ridiculous I am going to sound. "There was fresh blood on the ground leading out of the broken back door. I thought Zoa might have still been alive. It was a trap though."

Professor Heathrow holds his hand up and I pause. "What makes you think it was a trap?" He questions gently leaning forward in my seat.

"Zoa had been dead a while. There were old wounds on her arms with clotted blood and a newer wound that was still slowly seeping blood." I look to all the Professors and the Dean, they nod at me and I continue. "When I went to run away, nine other Flickers jumped out of the woods around me. They lured me right into the center of an ambush." I rub my forehead at my own stupidity. "I don't know if this is common knowledge of not, but Zoa, I mean, the Flicker, spoke to me."

"What was said?" Professor Heathrow asks very loudly.

"She asked if I had come for her. That was it." Professor Heathrow's glowing purple eyes glow brighter and he scribbles in his journal.

"How did you get away from ten Flickers?" Professor Julia asks, her Professor Alister and Locke all lean forward in their own chairs.

"I honestly got my ass kicked." I laugh. "If it wasn't for my haywire magic, I would have been a goner. I used enough voltage to kill a horse and the Flickers just shrugged it off." My gaze falls on each of them respectively. "If your students in the War program can't kill a bear with ease. Then should be on recon missions only." Everyone nods their heads. "My magic was slower to engage the more Flickers were biting me at the same time. I think four was my limit, if one more had latched on, I'd be dead." I rub my eyes trying to remember the rest and it hits me. "I also think I cleansed their souls after."

Professor Heathrow drops the cup in his hands and stares at me. "Explain. Flickers don't have souls."

"My Quintessence activated when I brought everyone back to the scene and I saw ten pink souls. I held their Soul Cords in my hand and pulled. Their souls changed back to their original colors and faded from view." I rub my eyes more vigorously, a headache forming then disappearing when my earring heats. "I don't really understand it myself Professor. I was hoping to talk with you more about it during our training." I look around the table and finish. "When I saw their souls revert I couldn't leave them as they were. I had Prince Silas burn then in a Flame Burial."

"Thank you." Dean Whyriss says when I finish. "You all will attend classes after lunch." She claps her hands together and I groan internally.

"Apologies Dean, but my Quint won't be attending classes today. One of our members almost died again, we will rest and attend tomorrow." Silas surprises me by speaking against the Dean, less surprising is the other three nod along with him.

Dean Whyriss scans each of us, her glowing blue eyes lingering on the bags under my purple eyes. She nods.

"Meeting end at 09:52." Professor Locke calls out.

The six of us stand and walk out. Ray breaks off from our group when we get outside and we continue home. Once the door to our house closes four sets of eyes fall on my causing me to roll mine.

"We can talk I promise, but first I need sleep." I don't wait for an answer and brush past everyone heading up the stairs.

"Let him rest." I hear Kyro whisper to Silas, I think. "We can talk in a couple of hours."

Chapter 13: We're Terrible Spies

K yro Ecicordus Kazetani

Yesterday, Thursday Night In the EMC

My mind keep wondering bac to the couch when I healed Valdis. All of his injuries were conclusive of being attacked by the Flickers. Except his spine. There's something wrong about it. Yes he had fresh injuries there, but there were other really old ones too. Deep scars in his skin all the way to the bone. And there was something foreign too. Something that didn't belong, like the skin was trying to reject it.

I felt something similar Tuesday night when Lucian broke his enchantment but it was hidden behind the waves of pain pouring off him. Tonight I got a better feel of the foreign object but I still have no idea what it could be.

I don't know anything about Valdis except what the stupid tabloids say. Those same tabloids have blasted lies about the rest of us. From I've seen thought is that Valdis works hard and keeps to himself. He would rather suffer in silence than tell anyone of his pain.

That's when it hits me. The four of us will have to figure out what he's hiding ourselves because Valdis will never tell us what's going on.

Valdis whispering to Ray causes me to lean my head back against the leather seat and feign sleeping. I can feel his gaze brush over my face before whispering again with Raymond. The EMC pulls over and Valdis shuffles over Callum and out the door. I can feel Callum's amusement through the bond before I hear him move.

"Where do you think you're going?" Callum rumbles causing my eyes to open in curiosity. My gaze landing on glowing purple eyes then trail down his handsome face to where Callum grips Valdis's arm.

Valdis speaking causes my eyes to snap back up to his face and I watch his as he tells Callum some lie. I know it's a lie because his face shows too much desperation to be anything else but a lie. There's fear in his eyes. Then the door cuts my gaze off and the EMC starts moving. I look over my shoulder and see his tall form through the back window and Valdis's shoulders sagging as we drive over the hill has me shouting.

"Stop!" I roar. Silas and Lucian, the only two not awake, jerk violently in their seats. "Stop the EMC. We're getting out." Three confused eyes fall on me and I just shake my head at the others. I'll tell them when we get out.

"If you insist." Ray shrugs and pulls over for the second time. We all pile out of the car and the others stand around waiting until we see the tail lights fade in the distance.

"What's going on?" Silas questions as I start walking back down the road where Valdis got out of the EMC. "Where's the Lazy Prince?" His footsteps right behind mine.

"That's what were going to find out." I call over my shoulder then turn back to the path looking for any sign that he walked this way. "Lucian?" I turn to the big guy. "Think you can track him?"

"Definity." He rumbles and steps in front of me, leading the way through the foliage.

"Kyro, what's going on?" Callum speaks this time, concern bleeding into his voice.

I pull the rubber band from my hair and retie the loose white strands away from my face. "Something isn't adding up and I'm tired of waiting for Valdis to tell us what's going on. I know we haven't told him much about ourselves either but I get the feeling that something is really wrong." Something is def wrong.

"Okay. Let's talk to him then get home. I don't want us to be late for the debrief." Silas nods at Lucian and we keep walking, this time in silence.

Some time passes before we see him. Standing all alone in a random clearing. Our silent plan is to fan out and surround him but I get too caught up in him when his hand trails down to his belt. I slip forward from my hiding spot and break a stick. I have zero time to react before Plasma scorches the earth three feet in front of me and a gasps escapes my throat. Holy fuck. I almost died.

Callum pops out of his hiding place first but I can't focus on any of their conversation. I really almost died. Valdis is actually a little scary. His glowing purple eyes keep tracking to my location and I move from my hiding spot.

"We just wanted to see what you were up to." I stalk over and lean against Callum. My heart pounding and I don't think I'll be able to keep from shaking.

You've been acting shady since you got here and we're getting to the bottom of this tonight." Silas call out and emerges form his own hiding spot.

Lucian follows next placing his hand on my shoulder and squeezing it in a comforting rhythm as we all standing around Valdis.

He keeps looking at his crystal watch and then at all of us frantically telling us to go. He's panicking. Bad. Something is very wrong. It's not until he tells us that we are going to die that I tune back into what's happening.

I grab Callum and Lucian and walk back to the tree line, Silas on our heels.

"There is no way that we're actually leaving." Silas growls at me. "I thought you wanted to see what he was doing?"

"I do but I think Valdis was being serious just now. Watch." I point back at Valdis and we watch him turn his back and place the belt between his teeth.

"What is he doing?" Callum leans against my back placing his chin on my shoulder and his hands on my hips.

I go to answer but can't. All of us gasp as we watch Valdis go rigid with pain. His muscles spasm and he falls to the ground. His body writhing. I hear a sob escape from Valdis but he presses his face into the ground to keep us from hearing any more.

"He's screaming." Lucian whispers. We all turn to look at him and his eyes are glowing more brightly than normal. "He's screaming into the earth." Lucian whispers again as if we didn't hear him the first time.

I turn my gaze to Valdis, his back twists and turns at impossible angles and then I see it. Through the tears in his combat uniform. The Iron Coffin.

"Oh my Gods." I go to run forward but Callum rips me back against his chest just as Valdis's magic erupts into the air in an electric dome. The white purple magic screams in a violent hum, screams out the pain he must be feeling. Tears track my cheeks.

"Kyro, what the fuck is that?" Silas grabs my shoulders and spins me to face the fire in his eyes.

They wouldn't know just by looking at it. It's been banned for over 400 years and only taught once in normal classes when talking about the histories of torture devices. Healers are taught about these devices more in depth because it's our jobs to help and heal people after they are subjected to them.

"It's the Iron Coffin." I turn back to Valdis and look inside myself grabbing the rope that represents our bond and measure his life energy, keeping my eye on it. "It was only supposed to be used on the worst of criminals about 400 years ago. The Iron Coffin was only ever used twice before it was banned, being marked as too brutal and too inhumane." The facts pour from my lips. "The victims of the Iron Coffin all died within a month of wearing it." Valdis is practically limp on the ground. His face still pressed into the earth.

"What does it do?" Callum asks and it's then that I notice how tightly he's gripping me.

"It rips the soul apart." I say to all of them.

"He said that he was diagnosed with a chronic illness three years ago." Lucian states placing his hands on mine and Silas's shoulders. "Do you think?" He trails off his own eyes on Valdis lying face down in the field. His magic lashing out around him.

"There's no way, the other two died within a month." I state staring at Lucian, he stares right back at me.

"Atlas had me make the earring over two years ago. Twins share a bond when their magic awakens." Lucian looks back to Valdis. "Haven't you wondered why Valdis is so good at shutting us out?"

Valdis's bond starts to grow weaker in my chest and a familiar full blown panic sets in. My eyes snap to where Valdis and I can barely see any breathing at all. "He's giving up." My hands squeeze Callum's where he holds me. "He's dying." I'm about to twist out of Callum's hold when everything stops.

I freeze and stare. Too scared to move and see that he's dead. Then he slowly pulls up to his knees and I watch as his head tilts back.

"Why won't you just kill me already?! Coward!" Valdis screams into the night with his more raspy than normal voice.

I'm sprinting before I know it. Sliding in front of Valdis and grabbing him. Pulling him into my chest, my magic running through his body. Healing anything I can. I don't care if I'm squeezing him too tight. He's alive. "Why didn't you tell us?" Is the only thing I can think to ask. He's obviously not okay.

"There is nothing to tell." Valdis pulls away from me all to soon.

We are going to talk about this. We have to. I'm not losing another bond member again. I can't. I won't. I don't care if I have to tie him down to a chair. We will be talkin about this. I'm tired of the secrets.

"We're going to be late." Valdis says snapping me out of my daze and I see he's talking to Lucian.

I make eye contact with Silas and we nod at each other in understanding. This conversation is not over.

Chapter 14: This Changes Nothing

Valdis Spyridon Aritiri

Friday, Present

A loud banging wakes me up from dreams best left untouched. My head lifts from my pillow and I glance at the crystal clock. 12:07.

The pounding continues and I roll out of my bed and walk over to the door. My oversized black hoodie drapes around my black joggers almost like a mini dress. I'm expecting to see Silas but instead Kyro stands in front of my door. His fist raised as if ready to bang on my door again. My eyes turn back to the clock then Kyro.

"I guess two hours is good enough." I press my palms into my eyes then push them back through my black and white curls.

"You need to eat and we're all going a little crazy waiting on you to give us some answers." Kyro shrugs then grabs my arm pulling me from my room and down the stairs. I can feel his magic seeping into me, looking for anything to heal. I don't jerk away from him this time. He already knows and I enjoy his touch.

Kyro pulls me into the living room and gently pushes me into one of the leather couches. Callum walks in from the kitchen and places a plate in my hands. He made a delicious smelling sandwich with a salad and he places a lemonade on the coffee table in front of me. Everyone else grabs food and sits around the living room. Kyro sits next to me and presses his thigh against mine. More of his magic flowing into my body.

"What do you want to know?" I rasp out. I honestly want to get this over with as soon as possible so I can go back to sleep. I looks like Silas is about to speak but Callum beats him to the punch.

"No." He states calmly. "Eat first. We all need our strength." Nods go around the room and we comply. Maybe a little awkwardly but Callum is right. At least he is about me. Kyro takes my plate from me when I finish my last bite and places it on the coffee table in front of me.

"Show us." Kyro comands me. His gold eyes staring straight into my soul. He leaves no room for argument and a sigh leaves my body. I spin around on the couch bringing my legs up and crossing them, giving the room my back. I reach my hand back and pull my hoodie up over my head but leave it around my arms and chest. My body may be that of a mans thanks to the enchanted ring changing my appearance but I am still a woman. It feels weird to show my chest even if my breasts are hidden by the enchantment. Gasps ring through the room at seeing my metal spine in proper lighting. Kyro may have been healing me this whole time but I'm positive that dried blood is still painted around the metal cuffs.

Kyro's hands find the bare skin on my back, I know it's him because I can feel his magic flow through me. "There's nothing to heal." I whisper to him. He's probably reaching his limit and I don't want him to waste his magic on me.

"There's blood on your back." He grits out. Frustration clear in his voice and tense fingers. "Obviously there is more to heal."

It's my turn to gasp when icy water runs up and down my metal spine. I shoot a glare over my shoulder at Callum his blue eyes glowing with power. "Valdis is right Kyro. It's dried blood." Kyro's hands trail between the metal cuffs sending a full body shiver through me and I pull my hoodie back on at lighting speed.

"How long have you had the Iron Coffin?" Lucian rumbles in his deep voice. His arm is wrapped around Callum with his hand resting on Silas's shoulder.

"Three years. It was my eaighteenth birthday gift." My gaze darts down to my hands and I pick at my hands. "A hell of a gift right?" I chuckle to myself.

"What did you do to deserve this punishment?" Silas asks and my eyes snap to him. Everyones eyes snap to him and I can see Kyro shaking his head at Silas. Does he really think anyone deserves this?

"Of course you would think the worst of me?" I want to be angry but the truth is that I did do something that day to deserve punishment but not this. Never this. "I killed a man that beating me to death." Now everyone is looking at me.

"Bullshit. What did you really do?" Silas scoffs. "A royal never would have been punished for defending themselves. Atlas never would have allowed it."

"Atlas didn't know." He couldn't have known. My eyes drift back down to my fingers and I continue to rip at my cuticles.

"How could Atlas not have know?" Callum asks cutting off Silas's accusations.

"We never got to meet." I can feel the tears well in my eyes but I refuse to let them fall.

"What do you mean? You were brothers." Callums head tilts in his confusion.

"We were kept apart after our parents death. It's an old custom among other things in the Kingdom of Souls to keep twins apart." I gloss over the part about twins with a female firstborn being abandoned or killed. I 'escaped' this fate by being royal, instead I was abused for twenty one years. "Atlas didn't know about my mistreatment because he wasn't told about it. No one was." I take a deep breath and continue. "I got the Iron Coffin when I killed one of the men who hurt me. They realized that my magic was stronger than expected and thought that the Iron Coffin was the best way to keep me in line. He was right." I rip a cuticle off and start bleeding but the pain is nothing compared to this story.

"How can I believe that the Lazy Prince was abused this whole time when there is evidence of you living it up in the tabloids all over the realm?" Silas runs a frustrated hand over the scruff on his jaw. "You see how your story doesn't line up right?"

"Lies." I swallow the scream of frustration in my throat. "Every single one of them was staged."

"Sure they were." It's in this moment that I realize that nothing I say to Silas will make him believe me. Not even seeing the Iron Coffin on my back. I can never trust him with my truth but I refuse to be seen as a liar.

I whip out my eCrystal and call Sin. She answers on the first ring. "Can I borrow Tardigrade? I promise to have her back in pristine shape Sunday night." I wait on her answer and thank her when she says yes. Sinclair pulls up about twenty minutes later and honks the horn on Tardigrade.

"If you want the answers you seek then follow me." I call over my shoulder. "If not then get fucked." I storm out the front door and head straight to Sinclair. She takes one look at me and then her arms are around me. Damn I really needed a hug. I throw my arms around her and squeeze.

"Are you okay?" She asks he face pressed into my chest.

"No, but I will be." The sound of the door slamming has me pulling away from Sinclair and getting in the drivers seat. I'm about to learn very quickly how to drive.

The doors to Tardigrade open and close. All the Princes are in the EMC and I start driving. No one comments on my very bad and very fast driving until we are well into the woods that I walked through on my escape.

"Where are you taking us? We've passed like eight signs that say do not enter." Silas grouches in the back seat.

"Shut up." I growl. "You'll figure it out when we get there." It probably isn't smart to be revealing so much to them but I'm so tired and I don't deserve to be called a liar when I'm finally telling the truth. Well most of it anyway. Actually just enough to get them off my back.

My gaze trails over to Lucian sitting in the passenger seat. "Can you track something from a little over two weeks ago?"

He guves me a curious look. Green eyes trailing up and down my face and rigid posture. "Maybe? Why?" His hand is firmly wrapped around the 'oh shit' handle.

"Because thats when I escaped." I go to say more but Silas cuts me off.

"Bullshit. Escaped from what? One of your whores?"

I ignore him and continue. "I'll drive us as close as I can remember but we will be on foot for a couple hours." My eyes remain on the road that I am driving entirely too fast down.

"I should be able to. I might need a power boost though." Lucian also ignores Silas.

"I have no problem with that if it means the royal dick has to eat his words."

We fall into silence for a couple more hours until I pull Tardigrade off the road and start driving her through the trees and foliage. We don't arrive to where I think is a good location until around 21:08. Everyone follow me when I get out of Tardigrade.

"This the spot?" Lucian asks. His braids clinking together as he look at the trees that look exactly the same as all the others we've passed today. I nod my head because it's as close as i'm going to get. Lucian holds his hands out to me and I place mine in his. His eyes glow a more briliant shade of green and I know my eyes are glowing brighter too. Lucian's eyes never leave mine but I know his focus is on the minerals all around us. "Got it." He lets go of me with one hand but keeps his hand around my other one. He starts walking and I have no choice but to follow. The other three close on our heels.

This keeps up for an hour and half before I see it and I freeze my hand slipping out of Lucian's. It was definitly a bad idea to come here. It was stupid. My breaths come in and out too quickly. I never should have done this. Fuck them. I had nothing to prove to them. My breathing is still too quick and I can't get a hold of myself. Warm hands wrap around my face and I'm met with blue eyes.

"Breathe with me." Callum places a hand on my male chest. "Follow my breaths." He lets go of my face and grabs my hand with his other hand and places it on his own chest. "In." He takes a breath. "Out." I do my best to follow his instruction and my breathing calms. I pull away from him and look at the ground.

"Sorry." I can't believe I had a panic attack in front of all of them. They did see me being tortured so I guess I shouldn't be that worried about it. "Lets continue." Callum has a sad look on his face but I don't want his pity.

I lead the others to the edge of the crater. It looks like no one has been here since I destroyed it. Good. No one should bother us.

Looking down into the crater reveals the levels underground. If I hadn't blown it up then it would just look like the woods. Everyone is blissfully silent as I lead them down to where I was kept. The compound isn't very big but my memories here are. There are only three room that I need to go to and only two of them that they need to see. I drop by the office first and start going through files that I think will be useful for Sir Howin to go through.

"What are you doing?" Kyro asks over my shoulder while I'm going through a cabinet.

"Gatherign evidence." Is all I say and continue with my task. I'm surprised when Kyro, Lucian and Callum start going through the other cabinets. Silas leans against the doorframe and doesn't help. He still thinks I'm a liar and I think the other three are just humoring me.

"Grab anything that might be incriminating?" Callum asks and I nod. "Who exactly are we looking for? You never said who hurt you."

"It doesn't matter, it's my problem to take care of." I pull more files from the cabinet.

"Because there isn't a name. He's abviously taking us on a wild goose chase because he doesn't want to tell us why he deserved the Iron Coffin." Silas remarks rudely.

"You do understand that the Iron Coffin is banned right. Silas, no one has ever deserved the Iron Coffin." Kyro snaps at Silas. I have never heard Kyro snap at Silas and it's a little unnerving.

"Whatever." Silas looks away from Kyro. "Are you guys done look at papers?"

A sigh leaves me and I nod. "I think so. Lets get on with the tour."

I wind through the underground halways/tunnels until we get to my room. It's mostly intact except for the ceiling and a wall. I refuse to walk in the room and hand back while the others walk in. Silas's orange eyes glow brighter and his and lights up with flames. Light shines over my cage and the others look around in confusion and slight horror. I think they know what this room is. Lucian kneels down and his eyes glow brighter as his hands press into the ground.

"This was your room?" Lucian questions. He already know the answer and when I nod his face crumbles. "How long?"

"As long as I can remember." I state simply. My gaze drifts over to where Silas's goes through the wardrobe.

"These are all the outfits you wore in the photos." I can't bare to look at the clothes a moment longer.

"Only in the photos were those wretched clothes worn." I state. "Burn them." The room brightens as he liht the clothes on fire and then dims once he's done. I don't know if he believes me yet but he will. "Come on." I head down the hall. "There's one more room you need to see. Then we can leave." I take them to the last room on my list, the torture room.

My eyes trail around the room, it wasn't touched in my blast. The place looks the same as it always did, maybe a little brighter thanks to Silas's flame. I can't help the tremmors that run through my whole body when

I look at the different devices and rigs they used when torturing me. I see Luciand kneel and start to use his magic.

"No!" I shout at him but I'm too late. His hand connects with the ground and his magic activates. I rush over to him and knock him away from his postition. Lucian looks at me with horrror. He sprigs to his feet and grabs me by the biceps.

"What the hell were all those emotions I felt. Valdis did they touch you?" All I can do is shake my head at him. He wasn't supposed to find out about this. No one was ever supposed to find out about this. "Did they rape you?" Lucian looks absolutely livid at the tears that are running doen my cheeks.

"You weren't supposed to do that." Is all I can say. My back presses into the wall gently, Lucian having pushed me back against it.

"Answer my question." He growls at me. Everyone else is silent waiting on my answer.

"Only the leader did. He lost interest when I turned eighteen." I close my eyes so I don't have to see the disgust on all of their faces. "The others weren't allowed to have me, I was only for him. His little g-" I cut myself off remembering that I'm supposed to be a boy. "His little boy." I shake my head at myself. "He stopped hurting me himself when I wasn't so little anymore. Instead he enjoyed watching the others beat the hell out of me." I pull out of Lucian's grip and head out the door. "I don't want to be down here anymore." I wind through the hallways and out through the hole I made in the earth. I don't care if they follow me or not. I'm leaving.

I find my way back to Tardigrade and climb in the back. I rest me head back against the seat and close my eyes. It's best I don't drive right now. I hear multiple doors open and shut.

"If we don't get back to the house before 00:00 pull over into a secluded area. I'm going to take a nap until then."

"Okay Valdis. Get some rest." Callum says from beside me. "We will pull over." The EMC starts moving and I fall into sleep that I wish was peaceful but isn't.

~~~~~~~~~~~~~~~~

(Sorry for the late update! I started a new job and haven't made the time to write. I'll do better once I get my routine. Have a great day/night!!!)
~~~~~~~~~~~~~~~~

Chapter 15: What Is Our Plan

Callum Vanrose Irvine

Friday Night, Present

Valdis is sound asleep on my shoulder, his breath tickling my neck every time he breathes. I can't help but to wrap my arm around him and hold him a little closer. It almost feels like I have Atlas back. I know I don't but it feels just as nice.

Lucian's green eyes find mine in the review mirror of the EMC, and I can see a soft smile curve his full lips. He knows exactly what I'm feeling. They all do.

Silas breaks the silence first. "I don't know if I believe him yet, but we are going to help him." He whispers shocking the hell out of me. Shocks all of us, disbelieving looks are on everyone's faces. "I may not like the Lazy Prince, but he is a part of this Quint." Silas nods his head up and down, as if he's trying to convince himself that this is a good idea.

"So what's the plan? Hope that he trusts us enough to tell us who has been hurting him all this time?" Kyro snarks in a whisper. "I don't know if you've been paying attention Silas, but we haven't been very welcoming. I doubt he tells us a thing more than he already has." I can't help but agree with Kyro. There is no chance in hell that Valdis will talk to us.

"We only know this much because we intruded on his privacy." Lucian rumbles lowly in his delicious deep voice.

"And for good reason that we did." Kyro jumps in. "It's going to kill him. The Iron Coffin. I don't know how he's survived this long and I don't know when his luck is going to run out, but it will."

"It's because he's strong." All eyes fall on me after my statement. It just slipped out without thought but I realize in this moment that it's the truth. He is strong, stronger than we give him credit for.

"No way-" Silas starts but I cut him off.

"Whatever stigma you want to have about Valdis needs to end. The facts are someone hurt him, badly I might add. He is a part of this Quint wether we wanted him to be or not. He is here." I take a deep breath to keep myself from yelling. "Nothing else should matter except that he is here."

"But Atlas-" Again Silas tries to start but I stop him.

"Atlas made his choice. A choice that he didn't trust us with." I rub my eyes with my free hand, trying to alleviate the stress. "It's time we started living with it instead of blaming the one person who couldn't have done anything to stop it." My attention falls to Valdis when I feel him shift against me in his sleep. His whole body shifts closer into me and I can't help but hold him that much tighter. Wether he knows it or not, I have his back. From this moment forward. I just hope the others have it too.

Chapter 16: I Know This Plan is Shit

V aldis Spyridon Aritiri

Saturday Morning, Present

The smell of bacon and eggs pulls me from my sleep and I wander down the stairs and enter a full kitchen. The conversation that was happening moments before I entered ceases completely. Orange, gold, green and blue eyes follow my movements as I make a plate and sit in my designated seat. I'm three bites into my meal before I give up.

"What?" The attitude pours from my mouth. It's supposed to be my weekend to relax and instead I'm being watched like some sort of side show. It's annoying.

"How did you sleep?" Callum asks and I can't help but remember waking up in the back seat of Tardigrade basically laying on top of him. Then I promptly was tortured for an hour then we drove the rest of the way back to the school.

"Fine..." My cheeks heat at the little smirk my answer puts on Callum's lips. "I'll probably be getting more now since I won't be sneaking out anymore."

"You were sneaking out?!" Silas booms sending a whole body flinch through me. "Why? With who? When?" His forearms bulge as he leans across the table to get in my face. Kyro's slender fingers rest on Silas's chest and pushed him back down into the seat.

"Uh... I was going into the woods... So you wouldn't hear me scream every night..." My eyes lock onto my eggs. "I didn't want anyone to know. Still don't actually." Gods can I shut up already? "I can keep doing that if it'll bother you guys. I was planning on going into the basement but if that isn't okay I can go to my spot in the woods." I turn and look to my left where Lucian is seated and tentatively find his eyes for a moment before looking back down at my plate. "I was actually wondering if you could make a silencing crystal? Or if you know where I could purchase one? My Knight and I haven't had much luck finding one."

A hand touches my chin and guides my face to look at Lucian's. "I can make you one after breakfast." Lucian releases my eyes and chin then looks around the others at the table. "It's a high grade enchantment so I'll need the entire Quint to help me make it." Nods go around the table.

A slight breeze fills the room then concentrates on my chin forcing it up and over to look at Kyro across the table. His golden eyes glow brightly with his power. "How much sleep have you been getting?" His question takes me off guard.

"Enough. I've been getting a nap in at lunch on most days." I try my best to shrug off the question. All the apparent concern and possible kindness from everyone is weirding me out a little. At this point their indifference or hatred is expected. Not what ever this is.

"That's not what I asked." Kyro's long white hair blows slightly in the breeze and his eyes harden on me.

"Around ten hours." I say thinking back on shower times and not including my naps because they really don't count.

"How are you getting ten hours of sleep a night? Our schedules don't allow that kind of time. Unless you're skipping out on your studies?" Silas questions. When I try to look over at him the air on my chin tightens.

"Go on." Kyro commands me.

"A week." My statement falls flat. My eyes rolling into the back of my head. "I get ten hours of sleep a week." The breeze holding my chin vanishes causing my eyes to snap back to focus on Kyro. He stands with purpose and rounds the table. Callum moves from the seat to my right and Kyro takes his place. "What are you d-"

My sentence falls silent when Kyro grabs the leg of my chair and spins it around to face him. He traps my knees between his own then grabs my face in his hands. Kyro's eyes light up and his healing magic flows through me. Callum steps to Kyro's back and places his hands on his shoulders, his blue eyes glowing brightly at sharing his power with Kyro.

I can feel their magic poking around my head. It doesn't feel as pleasant as it did before, but it doesn't feel bad either. Just foreign. It jars me when Kyro pulls back suddenly. "What the fuck Valdis." Kyro's hostile tone shocks me after he was so close to my face. "Your body is on the verge of shutting down. Why have you only been getting ten hours of sleep a week? This isn't sustainable." Kyro's hands fall to my knees where he grips me tightly waiting on an answer. "Tell me your whole schedule from start to finish right now." His grip and tone leave no room for argument.

"My day starts at 04:00 when I get up to shower and change for classes from 05:00 to 17:00. After classes I come back to the house around 17:20 unless

I study at the library or visit Atlas. If I do that then I get back around 19:30. Then I eat till around 20:30. After I head to my room and do class work or go through files until 23:00 when I sneak out and walk about forty minutes into the woods. We all know what happens from 00:00 to 01:00. It usually takes me around an hour to get back in my room. Finally I crash face down into my bed and pass out until it starts all over again." Kyro looks pissed after my explanation. They all kind of do actually.

"Dude, you have like a five hour window after class. Why aren't you taking a nap then?" Callum looks genuinely confused when he asks. I can't help but look down at my hands and twist a loose thread on my black jacket.

"I had to study, and I couldn't risk sleeping through an alarm. I'd wake everyone up with my screams. And I'd also probably set the house on fire. I wouldn't have been able to lie my way out of that. Staying awake was easier than anyone finding out my secret." I'm brought out of my word vomit by Kyro's thumbs running circles on my inner knees. I can't help but notice how nice they are. Long and slender but big an masculine at the same time.

"Are you ever going to tell anyone about your abuse?" Kyro asks gently. "Maybe the council could help you get justice?" His voice and body language is soft but all I see is Regent Lukadious's face. Sitting on the very Council that Kyro is speaking about.

"NO!" I'm flying backwards out of my chair and falling basically into Lucian's lap. His muscular arms catch me easily. "No, I have my own plan to get justice." My head shakes back and forth franticly. "No one can know." I'm thrashing in Lucian's grip now and the bastard holds onto me easily. "You can't tell anyone. Please." The beg falls from my lips and I look to Silas.

"Why?" His orange eyes hold mine. "Would you really rather everyone believe the lies that have been told for years?" Silas cocks his head to the side.

Lucian's arm still bands around me, still keeping me locked against his body. "Yes!" Despair falls from my lips. "I'd rather them believe anything but the truth." The rasp in my voice gets thicker with my emotion. "Once I finish my plan, the rumers and lies should all go away." I turn my head to look at everyone except Lucian who still holds me. "Let me take care of this myself."

"Tell us the plan, and if it's good enough then we will let you go through with it." Callum speaks causing me to turn to him. He's giving me an out so we can be done with this wretched conversation. My reputation shouldn't concern them.

"I only have a couple months before our... before my twenty-second birth-day." My body goes a little limp in Lucian's grip. "Once that happens I'll be able to ascend the throne and punish how I see fit. If I can find something that connects him to a significant enough crime, then I can execute him." A huge sigh leaves me and I sag even more into Lucian and stare at the black sun inked on my right palm. "My knight has been looking through files that Atlas started collecting after he figured out what was happening to me. Well, most of what was happening to me." I can't bring myself to tell them that the Flicker attacks probably have something to do with Regent Lukadious as well. I have no proof and it isn't relevant.

"Your plan sucks." Callum is the first to respond even after he was the one to give me an out. "It only works if you can find something."

"I know." Now I'm completely limp. Lucian is the only thing keeping me off the floor. "I never thought I would escape so I've only had a little over two weeks to come up with a plan. I'm honestly winging... well everything. Plus I'm basically doing this on my own, of the two people I've told only one of them knows everything and he's loyal to me by bond." All eyes fall to the black sun on my right palm. Everyone knows it's part of a master-servant bond.

Kyro scoots his chair forward and places his hand on my knee. "Why do you think you have to do this on your own? Why can't you trust us?"

My glare makes Kyro look away in an almost guilty way. "No one looked for me. No one asked questions. No one suspected anything was wrong. No one cared. And no one saved me. Except Atlas." Lucian lets me stand and take a couple steps away turning my back to all of them. "Except someone I've never met or will be able to meet. Atlas was the only one, and not even he believed something was wrong until our bond formed on our eighteenth birthday." I realize that my arms are bound tightly around myself. Trying to physically hold it together. "How can I do this any other way except alone?" Be your own hero.

"We're trying to help." Callum whispers but I refuse to look back at him.

"I may not have much experience with helping people or being helped, but I know this is not the way to do that." My arms tighten around myself as misery swells my body. "You don't accuse them of lying. You don't make threats against them. You don't ignore the words they say. You don't blame them for things out of their control." I'm done with this conversation and my footsteps take me to the kitchen door. "I'm leaving."

"Like hell you ar-" Silas tries to roar but I spin back towards him, plasma racing across my shoulders.

"I'm leaving!" I shout into the room. Stricken looks mark all of the Prince's faces. I take a second to breath and put my magic away. When I speak again, it's in a much calmer voice. "I will be back later." I spin on my heel and walk out of the kitchen then turn back around and storm back in. Lucian immediately catches my eyes and tilts his head causing his braids to clink together. "Where are the keys to Tardigrade?" Lucian says nothing just reaches into his pocket and pulls the keys out throwing them to me. "Thanks." For the second time I spin on my heal and walk out the door.

I don't stop until I'm behind the wheel and driving to the house Atlas rented.

Sir Howin greets me at the door. His beard as scruffy as ever. Bags under his eyes. And a smile so bright that it melts the trials of this morning away. "It's good to see you Princess." He places his fists toghether and bows. "Souls be safe." He greets.

I copy his motion and bow back to him. "Souls be safe." My smile is now just as bright as his. "It's always the best part of my life to see you Sir Howin." He ushers me into the house and shuts the door behind us.

"The place is secure if would like to get more comfortable." He assures me and I take a breath of relief. I remove the gold ring from my right hand and my true feminine features emerge from behind the enchantment. My long curly white hair falls to my waist and my curves fill out the places where my masculine facade fades. "I shall say again, it is good to see you Princess."

"Thank you, it has been too long since I've been able to wear my real skin." I say in a higher octave than my male enchantment lets me. It really is nice to be able to be me in rare moments like this.

Sir Howin and I walk into the living room still scattered with boxes and paper. That's when my quintessence decides to make and appearance. My purple eyes glow a brilliant shade and I zero in on Sir Howin's sunshine soul. The hints of purple allow me to know that he's from my Kingdom.

"Is something troubling you?" I ask as I take a seat on the sofa that is more paper than couch. "Your soul seems troubled."

Sir Howin sighs and takes a seat next to me. "I'm afraid the news I have isn't good." He sets his jaw and looks to me. "None of my leads have panned through." The weight of disappointment crushes me and I deflate on the sofa. "There's more. The Flickers aren't just attacking randomly, they are searching for someone and I think that person is you. Young women and men matching your age are disappearing all over the realm. It is only people matching your age." Sir Howin takes a deep breath. "Only we know who is commanding the Flicker and only we know who they're really looking for."

"This may be callous of me but I refuse to hand myself over to the Regent. If he would consider going to such lengths then it is safe to say he want's me for something much worse and it isn't my death. If he wanted me dead then he would have kill me with the Iron Coffin already." I rub my chin in thought.

"I agree with your assessment Princess. I think under no circumstance should you allow yourself to be captured. I also think you should bring your Quint into the fold." Sir Howin's brown eyes refuse to leave mine.

"I refuse." My raspy voice is strong in my conviction. "They were my brother's Quint and I refuse to put them in harms way."

Sir Howin jumps up from the sofa and rushes over to a filing cabinet in the corner. He tears through the paper and folders like a crazy man. "They were never supposed to be Atlas's Quint." He says over his shoulder.

"What do you mean?" The question is out of my mouth before I can stop it and my heart starts racing.

"The Quint is used a treaty between the five realms as a promise to never go to war." He says as he keeps going through the files at lightning speed. "I swear I just organized this." He mutters to himself.

"Right." I agree with him. This much of the treaty is common knowledge. "But what did you mean that the Quint was never Atlas's?"

"Aha!" Sir Howin shouts and runs back over to me with an old yellow paper in hand. "What I mean is," the paper is thrust into my hands. "The treaty clearly states that it must be preformed between firstborns. Atlas's was the second born child. You are the firstborn twin. The Quint was always supposed to be your's, not Atlas's."

The paper falls from my hands and the world bottoms out from beneath me. My head falls into my hands and my breathing increases along with my heart rate. "They were always supposed to be mine?" I already know the answer but I need Sir Howin to say it all the same.

"Yes." He makes the answer simple for me and I love and hate him for it.

"But Atlas was so happy with them. I could feel it through the bond. He was happy." I'm rambling at this point. "The Gods blessed his Quint. It was his."

"The Gods often work in ways that confuse mortals like us. My belief was that Atlas was supposed to hold onto the Quint until you could get to them." The tears are falling before I know that I'm crying and then I'm pulled into the arms of Sir Howin. He says no more about the matter and lets me pour my feelings into his chest. After I've had my satisfying cry I pull back and look at him. "Onto other matters?" He questions.

"Yes." I answer in a still wobbly voice.

"I think the only way that we will be able to catch Regent Lukadious is to catch him in the act." Sir Howin exclaimed.

"How? If I get within a hundred feet of him then he will sense the Iron Coffin and find me. Plus I can't be more than a couple miles from my Quint before that wretched tug tries to pull me back to them." I couldn't ask Sir Howin to do it. He's been a retired knight for too long. Just when I'm about to ask if there was someone we could hire the door bursts open and in walks Sinclair. The ring was halfway back on my finger but I pull it back off. Sin knows basically everything.

"Did you miss me?" She asks carrying coffee.

By the time I've finished explaining the plan to Sin she's already on the phone trying to get on a school sanctioned mission at the last location someone went missing from. It's in a small town in the Kingdom of Runes, and it looks like she will be leaving in the morning.

A bad feeling crawls up and down my spine but I have no choice but to let Sinclair go on this mission. She will hate me if I don't let her and I can't have the one person I care about at the school hate me.

Chapter 17: Maybe Things Are Changing

Valdis Spyridon Aritiri

Saturday Night, Present.

After an impromptu going away dinner for Sinclair I find myself standing in front of the door to the Quint house. Staring. Sin has long left after dropping me off with promises to swing by in the morning for a proper goodbye hug. The ring that is enchanted to make me look like a boy is back on my left thumb. I'm about to open the door when searing pain tears through my soul. Panic shoots through my body and my eyes lock onto my crystal watch. 23:00 hours. My torture session is starting a whole hour early.

One hand on the door and the other hand on the knob keeps me from falling over from the initial shock. I think he might actually kill me. I can't do this here. Not out in the open. I force myself to turn the knob and I fall ungraciously through the doorway and crash into the foyer. A pot shatters against the floor along with the table in the foyer.

I do my best to crawl past the mess I made and a sharp pain slices into my knees. I definitely sliced them open on the pot. That doesn't matter right now though. What matters is getting down to the basement. My crawl to the basement door is slow and torturous as the pain continues to increase in my soul. It's hard to see where I'm going through the tears but I've been living here long enough to get there with my eyes closed.

Once I'm at the door I reach up and open it and drag myself through the door. There's not enough room for me to close it unless I take a step down but when I go to do that I lose strength and fall all the way down the steps, hitting ever edge on the way down. All I can do is groan before I start to drag myself away from the steps and to the farthest corner of the stone basement. I can't remember why it's strange that I can drag myself in a straight line and then it hits me. Where is the hot spring? My face pressed against the cool stone and I can hear water bubbling from underneath. Lucian must have covered it after I left. I'll have to thank him tomorrow.

I crawl to the center of the room before the pain really sets in. I don't have the energy to find something to bite onto so I settle for my jacket. It does little to muffle me and I have to hope that no one hears me. My plasma shoots out from my body like an electric tree when the Iron Coffin settles on a level of suffering that I'm not used to. I really think the Regent is trying to kill me this time.

Just when I think I've settled into the pain it amps up another notch and a raspy scream tears from my throat. I can barely hear the sounds of footsteps coming down the stairs over my own screams and the violent hum of my magic.

"What the fuck? What time is it?" One of the Princes asks and I can't tell who's speaking over the pain and humming.

"It's 23:28." Another answers.

"I thought the sessions only happened between 00:00 and 01:00?" Another voice asks.

"This is bad. This is really really bad." Another voice.

I can't tell if everyone is talking or if it's one or two. All I know is that this is probably going to kill me. I thought the Regent need me alive. All the data till now suggested that he did, but I guess he's changed his mind. Then the pain intensifies and I can think no longer, just an animal being tortured in a cage.

"Valdis!" The voice sounds irritated and angry. Like they have been calling my name for a few minutes. I look up through my tears and find gold eyes inches away from my face. "Breathe!" Kyro yells in my face. "Fucking breathe!"

I didn't realizes that I had stopped breathing before but my diaphragm suck oxygen back into my lungs. My eyes still on Kyro. Kyro who is way too close to me. Kyro who is within range of my plasma. I spit the jacket out of my mouth. "Go." I force the word to form in my mouth. "I don't wanna hurt you."

"I'm staying." Kyro says. "If you go, I go." And then he places his hand on mine and my heart stops. My plasma brushes up against Kyro at an incredible speed then bounces off him and redirects. Kyro smiles to himself then pulls me against his muscular body. His magic flows into me healing the damage I caused myself getting down here. One hand runs through my hair as his other holds me close to his chest. My screams are muffled by his body. I startle slightly when another body brushes against my back and presses me further into Kyro. When I try to turn my head Kyro holds my head tighter. "It's Callum." Kyro says in my ear as another wave of pain pulses through my soul.

"I'm alright. You didn't hurt me." Callum says in my other ear as he snakes his arms around my masculine chest and rubs his hand over my heart. "I'm alright." He says again.

Throughout the session my head is ripped back by my hair a couple times and Kyro shouts in my face to keep breathing. It's only when we move into the second hour that two more bodies join our weird body sandwich. Time feels like it doesn't move at all until it's finally over and I can feel all the hands providing me some semblance of comfort. I unclench my hands from Kyro's shirt and I hurts to relax them. I open my eyes to look down and my finger and see blood covering the tips.

"I hurt you?" My voice is absolutely raw and more tears stream down my face. Callum pulls my back tight against his chest, his hand still rubbing over my heart.

"Just a scratch. Nothing I didn't heal immediately." Kyro gives me a small smile and slides his hands from my back to rest them on my thighs that are on either side of his waist. A sliver of air keeping this almost decent. "Valdis, I thought you said the sessions were only an hour. From 00:00 to 01:00?" Kyro's question snaps my head out of the gutter.

"I think he's angry that I haven't come back." My thoughts are running a mile a minute but I don't have the energy to formulate a single one of them. All I know is. "I can't do that again." I hiccup a sob Callum tightens his grip resting his head where my shoulder and neck meet. "I can't." I press the palms of my hands into my my eyes to try and physically hold the tears back. I know it's not considered manly to sob but I'm not a man, not really, and the need for men to hide their emotions is stupid anyway.

It's like a damn breaks inside me and the barriers I put up inside myself shatter. I can feel when it happens, everyone stiffens at the exact same time. The bond just opened. Full stop. No warnings.

"Valdis?" Lucian's voice is crushed. The pain in his voice snaps me out of it and I start putting the barriers back up. Callum's hand stops rubbing my heart.

"Stop." He says into my neck.

"I'm trying." I whisper as I keep building my walls.

I can feel Lucian scoot even closer and grab my wrists pulling my hands away from my eyes. I have no choice but to look at him. "Callum mean's for you to stop building your walls. Quints are meant to share their emotions."

"I can't do that either. No one should be forced into this dumpster fire." I pull my hands back from Lucian and slowly untangle myself from the four of them. I refuse to look in any of their eyes. "Thank you all for being there for me. I'll clean my mess up in the morning." I"m to the steps when Lucian calls to me.

"We're going to fix this Valdis. Just give us time."

I can't tell if he's talking about the bond or about the Iron Coffin but my answer to both is the same. "You can't." I duck my head and race up the stairs to my room and soak it with my tears because I wan't more than anything to fix all of this.

~~~

My alarm goes off the next morning and I forget for a moment why I set it before it hits me and I'm racing down the stairs not caring how much noise I make. I throw the front door open and meet Sin in the middle of the walk way. I swing her around and she giggles.

"I thought I was gonna have to knock on the door." She laughs and punches me in the arm when I set her down.
~~~

"You almost had to." I laugh right along with her. My eyes fall on Tardigrade. An empty Tardigrade. "You're going solo?" I shout the question at her. "Did the Professors not listen to a word I said during the debrief?"

"Cool your jets Val. I'm only riding up there solo. I'll meet up with a team in the region so I won't actually be alone. I should get there Tuesday morning." She grins at me. "There's nothing to worry about and I promise to check in every night if it makes you feel better?"

"Make it breakfast, lunch and dinner and I promise not to worry as much." I give her a sheepish grin.

"Deal." She says easily. "Fair warning though. The service between Kingdoms is shit but I will do my best to get a message through. But I do swear to call you when I meet up with the team."

"Okay. I will be patient, but if I don't get a call Tuesday then I will be calling your dad." I give her my best stare down to let her know I mean business.

Sin groans so loud that I sweat the Gods themselves can hear her. "Fine." Sin's purple eyes glance over my shoulder and I know the Princes are there before she can say anything. I swoop in and give her a kiss on the forehead. It's so cutesy.

"Promise you'll be careful." I pull her into another hug.

"I promise." Sin gives me one last squeeze and turns to climb into Tardigrade. I don't look away from my bestfriend until she's driven out of sight, then I turn back and face the four Princes. Callum has a nasty look. Lucian looks disappointed. Kyro looks away. And Silas looks like normal, pissed. All four of them stand there in shorts or pj pants and nothing else. I find it very difficult to keep my eyes off their muscular chests.

"What?" I ask before making my way back to the front door where they all stand.

"You really had to run down and out here just to give your girlfriend a hug?" Callum asks with as much attitude as any four year old that didn't get ice cream.

"We thought we were getting attacked or that you were having another impromptu torture session." Kyro says right after Callum finishes.

"What was that all about? It couldn't have just been because you wanted to see her." Lucian asks a decent question.

"Sinclair is meeting up with a team in the Kingdom of Runes." Silas's attention snaps to me. "She's supposed to meet up with them Tuesday morning and I wanted to say goodbye and tell her to be safe before she left."

"A mission?"

"A team?" Silas and Lucian question at the same time.

"All I know is that it's a recon mission in a small town off the border of our two Kingdoms." I say to Silas then turn to Lucian. "I am also not sure what team she's meeting up with but I do know that the Dean is sending her there and that the team works closely with Dean Whyriss." I look back and forth between the two of them. "Sin said she'd check in with me anytime she can find service."

"You know the service between Kingdoms is shit right." I nod at Callum even though he's being a dick. "You probably won't hear a thing from your girlfriend until Tuesday." Callum turns back to head inside the house. "I might as well make breakfast since we're all up." He snarks over his shoulder.

I lean towards Kyro and whisper. "What's his problem?"

Kyro shrug even though I suspect he knows the answer. "Callum doesn't like to be woken up early when he can sleep in." The answer is shit. No one likes to be woken up early when they are allowed to sleep in.

We all head inside and towards the kitchen where Callum is banging pots and pans together preparing breakfast. Everyone steps in a little tentatively and sits in their unassigned assigned seats. Maybe he really really doesn't like to be woken up. Callum is the first to break the awkward silence.

"Do you love her?" It takes me a second to figure out that he's talking to me but I answer after a few beats.

As a friend and Sinclair knows that. It might be okay to let the ruse drop. Then it hits me. Callum is jealous. Maybe I won't give up this ruse just yet. "Yes. I think I do love her." The words are out before I can completely think it through.

A crash sounds then vigorous cooking takes it's place. "Do you think or do you know?" Callum asks and I turn in my seat to look at him.

"I know. Sinclair has been there for me since I met her. The love thing just happened along the way." I do my best to hide my smirk when Callum winces. He doesn't know I mean as a friend.

"You know," Lucian starts, obviously trying to save Callum. "Quints usually discuss relationships together."

That was not the way to handle this. I'm pissed. "So now you all want to micromanage my relationships?" My tone has a definite 'don't go there' vibe.

"That's not what I meant." Lucian pinches the bridge of his nose. His braids are tied up in a knot on his head.

"What did you mean?" I bite out.

"There's usually an open discussion about the dynamic of the Quint and if you want to introduce someone into it. Like it or not, there are four other people attached to you and it's easier to have a discussion with any significant other or possible significant other to help them, and you, understand that this Quint isn't going away just because you meet someone you like." Lucian winces after he finishes. "I hope that sounded better to you than it did to me?" He shrugs his shoulders.

I start rubbing my temples to ease an oncoming headache. "No, you're right. It makes sense when you say it like that." My shoulders sag. I guess I should probably tell the truth if I want to avoid something messy in the fire. I really don't have time for messy. "Sinclair and I are just friends."

"I thought you two were dating?" Callum asks as he starts whisking eggs together aggressively. "Are the two of you just scratching an itch?" He frowns into the bowl after asking.

It takes me a second to understand what he's saying and my cheeks flame when I finally get it. "NO!" I practically yell. "Sin and I aren't intimate like that." My hands are shaking frantically in front of my face like I'm trying to wave the conversation away. "The plan was for us to fake date so people wouldn't be suspicious of why I can't actually flirt or hook up." Confused faces stare back at me. "Look. During my first extra lesson for my Quintessence it became very clear that I would not be able to hide my suffering from her or Professor Heathrow." Nods go around the table so I continue. "I told Sinclair everything about my time with the R- with the man who hurt me and about how I needed help looking like a playboy or whatever the tabloids liked to call me. Sinclair agreed to fake date me."

"So why did you just act like you cared about her?" Kyro asks while he pulls his long white hair into a ponytail. His brows scrunched together.

"It may have started as a cover but I would consider her as my bestfriend. Everything else I said about her is true. I do love her, she's my bestie. My first friend." My smile is so wide that my cheeks hurt then my smile falls. "I really am worried about her being gone though." I rub my chin vigorously then look to Silas. "I don't suppose I could ask you to have the Dean's team check in with you?"

Silas barley looks at me. "No."

I smack my palm with my fist. "Thought not." My eyes roll as disappointment settles into my stomach like a rock.

A large hand rubs my shoulder and I look over to Lucian. "Sinclair is a fifth year correct?" He clarifies then continues with whatever he was going to say. "Then she has had way more training than the five of us combined." He gives me a soft smile with his lusciously full lips. "She's also in the knights program and has trained exclusively with Professor Locke correct?"

I rub my chin thinking back on the conversations we've had. "She mentioned to me that he was her favorite instructor."

"Good. That means Sinclair knows how to take care of herself. Professor Locke would never allow one of his students into a situation they were unprepared for." Lucian's gentle rub turns into a light shoulder massage and I try to soak in the contact as discretely as possible.

A loud sigh sounds from across the table causing my eyes to snap open. I didn't know I had closed them. "If you haven't heard from her by Tuesday, then I will contact my knights and have them look into it." Silas mumbles out.

I'm holding Silas's hands before I realize that I'm halfway over the table but that doesn't matter. "Thank you. Thank you. I know you don't owe me anything but thank you."

Silas's orange eyes are practically bugging out of his head before he gives my hands a light squeeze and pulls back. "I think I might owe you more." He says under his breath but I hear him anyway.

Chapter 18: Open The Bond, Please

Valdis Spyridon Aritiri

Sunday Morning, Present

Breakfast is decently peaceful and we clean up after our meal while we let Callum sit out. The cook doesn't clean.

"Did you still want the silencing crystal?" Lucian grabs my attention when I hand him a plate to dry. "We didn't finish talking about it before you left."

I contemplate for a minute if I really need it anymore since they all know and the basement has decent noise cancellation but then memories of last night flood my mind. About how the session started early and lasted twice as long and then uncertainty floods my mind. The schedule has been set since I escaped. What if I can't predict when it happens anymore? My pulse races. What if he turns the Iron Coffin on whenever he feels like it. Blood roars in my ears. What if I can't get to a safe location? A plate shatters in my hands. What if there's people around and I hurt someone when I lose control of my magic? Crimson drips from my fingers. What if I can't get to the four of them? My legs give out but someone catches me before I hit the ground. I need them.

Everything is a blur but I can feel my knees press into something soft then my body is pressed into some else's, chest to chest. I think I'm straddling someone on the couch. Big arms wrap around me and rock me back and forth in small, soft motions. My face is pressed into a soft cotton shirt that smells like the woods and spice. It's a great scent. The scent makes me take slow, deep inhales so I can save it in my memories. The feeling of a strong steady heartbeat against my face coaxes my own heart to slow it's rhythm. I need them.

Warm hands pull mine away from where they clutch into the cotton shirt and I know Kyro is healing the cuts I got from when the plate shattered in my hands. I'm aware that it isn't Kyro's lap that I'm sitting on and Callum was too far away to catch me before I fell. It's Lucian or Silas. Strong arms still hold me tight. I guess it doesn't matter that I've calmed down enough, because these strong arms won't let go before I do. Or I hope they won't. I need them.

Kyro gives my hands back to me after he finishes healing them and I've decided that I've gathered myself enough to pull back. There is resistance from the whoever's arms I'm in but when I push back again he lets me. The hands attached to the strong arms move down my sides and grab my hips. I know this is as far back as I'll be able to pull away. A mere six inches.

I'm slow to pull my eyes up, away from the cotton shirt, and see whose lap I'm sitting on. I'm allowed to go at my own pace. So that rules out Silas. I'm not shocked when gold charms, woven and clasped through over forty braids wink at me from a topknot. Lucian waits patient for me to meet his green eyes framed by dark lashes. I slowly trail my eyes down to his strong brows then down the center of his freckled nose. I've never noticed them before, they're cute. My eyes fall to his full lips then I finally bring them up to his kind eyes. His thumbs rub gentle circle into my hip bones.

"Where did you go?" His voice rumbles softly and I can feel the vibrations through my whole body.

My eyes remain on his but I distract myself by tracing my fingers over the textured skin of new scars. I have to clear my throat before I can get the words to come out. "I can't predict him anymore." Is all I can say before I feel my chest tighten back up.

Lucians grip tightens on me. "Predict who?" He coaxes me.

I take a deep breath and keep my eyes focused on Lucian. He's keeping me grounded, present. "If last night wasn't a fluke then that means the schedule of when I get torture is no longer set." I practically wheeze the last words out and Lucian changes his tight grip and soothing circles for slow strokes from my hip to my knees. It distracts me from the panic.

"So that means he could activate the Iron Coffin whenever he feels like it?" Silas is the one to ask but I can't break my eyes from Lucian's or else I'll panic again.

"He always could but-" my throat freezes and again Lucian changes his pattern of comfort.

Callum finishes my sentence for me. "But you've been on a schedule for two weeks and thought it would stay that way."

"I have no idea when it'll be activated. Where I'll be when it does. How long it'll last or who will be around me." Tears roll off my cheeks and Lucian's hands freeze. "What if I can't find somewhere to hide? What if someone sees? What if I hurt someone?" My voice breaks and I have to regather myself. "I can't do it alone."

"You won't have to. We are with you in every class except for the two hours of core magic classes and your extra lessons." Kyro speaks softly, as if I'm some scared animal that's going to bolt at the first opportunity. He has a point because old me totally would, but new, well trying to be new, me won't. "Sinclair is with you in your extra lessons so that just leaves the two hours." Kyro reassures me.

"That's still two hours Kyro." My gaze still hasn't broken from Lucian. "A lot can happen in two hours. What if I can't reach you?"

Lucian's grip settles on my hips again and tightens. "Open the bond." He states simply. It is now that the bolting reaction that Kyro was worried about hits me full force and Lucian was ready for it. His grip on my hips keeps me for launching myself from his lap.

"I can't." I try to pry his grip off me but can't remove his hold. "I can't do that." I try harder to get out of his hold but it's like fighting against a damn tree. "I'm not ready to share everything with any of you."

"Valdis, look at me." Lucian's voice is soft but commanding and the stare that I didn't know I broke is back. Purple to green. "I'm not asking you to do that. I'm not asking you to open the bond all the way."

That statement makes me pause in my effort to escape. "The what do you mean?"

"Open it just a little. Just enough so we can check on your emotional state when it heightens." He's back to rubbing circles into my hipbones. "Enough so we know when you panic or are in pain. When we feel your spikes then we can get to you faster than if you told someone to get us or scrolled trough numbers on your eCrystal."

I take a second to think it over. It'll be difficult to be that precise with my control over my side of the bond but I think it could work. It definitely would be easier than telling someone to go get one of them. A small laugh bubble out of me causing Lucian to tilt his head in confusion. "It would be faster considering I don't have any of your numbers." A frown curls Lucian's lips.

"You don't have any of our numbers?" His fingers tense. "How?"

I give him an 'are you kidding me' look. "We all haven't exactly been besties since I got here. I'm pretty sure all of you are only being nice to me because you'll never be as cruel as him."

"That's not why Valdis." Warmth fills me. It's the first time Silas has used my actual name. Gods I feel stupid. "It's just come to our attention that you didn't deserve half the shit we threw at you." More like all of it.

"Where's your eCrystal? We're all putting our numbers in it." Callum states and I can see him moving around the living room out the side of my eye.

"Alright." I know it wasn't a question but I answer all the same. "It should be in the kitchen."

Callum leaves and comes back a second later with my eCrystal outstretched in his hand. "Looks like Sinclair messaged you." Callum rolls his eyes. I'm snatching it out of his hand a moment later and holding it between me an Lucian.

'I know it's only been like three hours since I left but I'm about to hit the edge of my range and wanted to let you know messages will be spotty from now till Tuesday. Love you babes'

The message was sent thirty minutes ago and I type out a reply lightning quick.

'Thanks for the update, the boys know we're not really dating... had to confess or else you'd have too meet them all and suffer through a conversation on future relationship expectations... so you're welcome! Love you always doll'

I don't get a response back and hand my unlocked eCrystal to Lucian. He frowns at my contact list. "You only have two people in here." Lucian gives me a confused look.

"Who's the second one?" Callum asks and sits next to Lucian sandwiching my left thigh between the both of them and looks at the crystal screen. "Who's Sir Howin? Some kind of companion worker?" Callum's jaw tightens and he gives me a cold look.

"He's my knight." I wave my right palm with the black sun on it in front of his face. His face softens and he grabs the phone from Lucian.

"I wasn't done putting my contact in there." Lucian rolls his eyes and looks over at Callum.

"I know. I'm going to put us all in there." A collection 'no's' ring for everyone except him. "Too late, I'm already done." He locks my eCrystal and hands it back to me. "If you guess us all correct on the first try then I'll make you anything you want to eat, deal?" He gives me a smirk.

"What happens if I lose?" I've been living off of the same food since I can remember.

"If you lose then you have to do each of us a favor. Deal?" He scoots over and presses my thigh harder into Lucian's.

"Make it four things I want and you have a deal." I hold my hand out but instead of taking my hand instead Lucian's grip tightens on my hips and Callum leans in super close to my face. I try to lean back but Lucian's hands prevent me from going anywhere.

"Why are you so close to my face?" I practically squeak when Callum stops an inch from me.

"Sealing the deal the traditional water way." Callum gives me a 'duh' look.

My hand lands on his chest to keep him from advancing any farther. "The Kingdom of Cures hasn't sealed a deal with a kiss in over two hundred years." I can feel everyone's eyes on me and my face and ears heat.

"I know, but there's something more fun about using the traditional style of sealing deals." Callum is not going to let this go so I lean forward lightning fast, give him a lil peck, and pull away before he can even blink. My lips come back moist and I lick him off my lips.

"Done." I ignore the heat my face is giving off and try to change gears. "Next topic." I demand. The golden and silver magic swirl the air between me and Callum. He looks just as confused as I feel and then the magic congregates over his lips and mine. When the magic fades from view a thin black line paints the center of Callum's bottom lip. "Callum?"

"Oh my Gods." Callum places his hand over his mouth and stares at my bottom lip and I just know that the same black line marks me too. My head is tilted to the right by Silas where he drags his thumb over my bottom lip. His eyes glowing orange with his magic.

"Callum, the seal is real." Silas's pissed expression isn't directed at me for once.

"I know it's real. I'm from the royal line." Callum quickly looks at me. "Valdis I was joking about actually sealing the deal the traditional way." It's Callum's turn my head an run his thumb over my bottom lip.

I pull my head back away from his hand so I can speak. "What does everyone apparently know that I don't know?" Callum rubs his hand down his face and his tan skin turns pale.

"This is about to be a whole history lesson." He grumbles.

"Just give me the cliff-notes then." I grumble back.

"Fine, the reason why deals where sealed with a kiss is because members from the royal family can make a deal unbreakable through the exchange of body fluids. Blood is acceptable but deeply frowned upon." He gives a full body shiver after the last part and I'm a little pissed that this isn't common knowledge but I guess every kingdom has it's own little secrets.

I try to alleviate the tension headache forming by rubbing my sinuses. "So what you're saying is that we have to honor all aspects of the deal or... what happens if we don't."

"Long story sort, you die." Callum says in a deadpan way.

"And, just so we're clear, no form of help can be given outside of the two of us?" Concern starts to flood my system. I just handed the four of them a ton of power and all I get out of it is four meals. Idiot.

"Correct. We didn't set a time limit but default time is one week." I'm almost too scared to ask my next question but I need the answer.

"If I don't complete my side of the deal then does that mean I automatically lose or do I die?" How do I get myself into these situations?

"You lose. The deal will rule in my favor." Callum's blue eyes look at anything except me.

"I guess there's nothing to be done about that now." I look back at Lucian. "Since we're all here, can we go ahead and make the silencing crystal?"

"Of course." He releases my hips and pulls some gold and a black crystal from his braids. "I need everyone to channel their magic into me. This enchantment requires a lot of magic and focus." Everyone crowds around Lucian and places their hands on him. "Valdis, this enchantment is specifically for you so I need you to cup my hands with yours and channel your magic that way." I nod and place my hands around Lucian's much larger hands.

Soon all of our eyes are glowing and magic floods into Lucian. It's an informal Quint circle where only one is getting the biggest magic boost of all time. I pour as much magic into Lucian as I possibly can. This enchantment needs to be perfect. It doesn't take long for the enchantment to finish and by the end we are all panting hard and shaking from depleted energy. Lucian is the first to move when he reaches up and tilts my head to the right exposing my left ear. I give him a nod and Lucian pierces my left earlobe. The pain lasts only for a second before the crystal in my right ear heats and takes the pain away. I do a little test wiggle of my head causing the dangling earrings to sway back and forth and determine that the weight feels the same on either side. I turn curious eyes to Lucian.

"The are the same in every aspect except the crystal color." Lucian explains, answering my unasked question. "To activate the crystal, tap it twice. To deactivate, tap it twice again." Lucian takes a breath. "You should know that the crystal won't work on the four of us."

"Simple enough and I understand why it won't work on y'all." I nod to him. "Thank you. Thank you all." I give a sad smile. "At least I'll have a little peace of mind now." It is now that I realize that I am still straddling Lucian's lap. I get up quickly this time and move away from the couch, slowly inching backwards towards the stairs. "I'm going to go to my room and try to get some more sleep." I awkwardly point my thumb over my shoulder and tuck my eCrystal into my pocket.

Silas gives a rare small smile. "I think we should all take the day to rest and catch up any assignments that we missed."

I quickly bolt up the stairs throw myself onto my mattress. Why were Lucian's thighs so thick and why did I like being pressed against him so much? And why were Callum's lips so sweet? My whole body is on fire and I'm feeling sensations I haven't felt before. Is this arousal? I've read about it but it hasn't really happened to myself. Now is not the time to be thinking about this. To distract myself I pull out my eCrystal and look at the names Callum put into my phone. Set my phone aside and stare at the wall for a minute. Then look again at the names Callum chose.

Chapter 19: Figured Out Who Made The Stairs

V aldis Spyridon Aritiri

Monday Morning, Present

A persistent knock sounds on the front door. I walk out of my room at the same time Kyro walks out of his. His white hair messy from sleep. I look down at my crystal watch and see the time is 03:00.

"Do you know what's going on?" He yawns and walks next to me down the stairs.

"No idea." I shrug as we meet up with the other three.

Silas opens the door then steps back as the Dean and her Quint force their way into our house. "I'm sorry but this couldn't wait till the morning." She says as she walks into the living room, all of us close on her heels. Dean Whyriss sets up an eTop on the coffee table and pulls up a news article.

"BREAKING NEWS: PRINCE ATLAS, FIRST BORN PRINCE OF THE KINGDOM OF SOULS IS RUMORED TO BE DEAD!

In more shocking news. Prince Valdis, second born Prince of the Kingdom of Souls is missing.

No one has seen the Lazy Prince since his last scandal over a month ago. Could Prince Valdis have something to do with Prince Atlas's death? A taskforce has been put together to find the missing Prince and uncover the truth.

CLICK HERE TO READ MORE"

My butt hits the seat after reading the article. "They think I killed him?" The question falls flat in our crowded living room.

"I'm afraid so." Dean Whyriss says in a concerned voice. "We currently have a media blackout and a barrier put in place." She starts. "But it will only last so long."

"Do they know that Prince Valdis is here?" Silas asks, his shoulders sag like the weight of the world rests on his shoulders.

"No, but it's only a matter of time." Professor Locke answers his Prince. "The world knew that Prince Atlas was studying here with his Quint, so it is only natural that this will be the first place they look." Professor Locke touches his lip then chest with two fingers in the traditional greeting to Silas.

The two of them keep discussing plans but I tune them out. He's gonna find me. My location will get out and the Regent will know where I am. He's gonna find me. Panic and dread pull me into a frozen state staring at the ground. All I can feel is the phantom pain of the beating I will get when he drags me back underground. My body shakes with the anticipation of each blow.

My attention is broken by someone kneeling in front of me. Professor Heathrow takes my hands in his. "What is the matter Prince Valdis? Your soul is all over the place." His purple eyes glow with his magic and I can see him studying the shape and color of my soul. It makes me curious as to what exactly he is seeing.

"I don't want to be found Professor. I can't be." My eyes lock onto his and I know he's connecting some dots about our study sessions and the pain he can feel in my soul.

"You cannot run from your pain forever." He says to me softly. "The pain will catch you when you are unprepared."

My hands clutch his harder. "What should I do? I'm not ready?" The fear is starting to strangle my breath. I allow the emotion to trickle through the Quint bond and can feel all four Princes move closer to me in a discrete manor. By Professor Heathrow clocks it. He has been in a Quint much longer than we have. A smile twinkles in his eyes.

"You must prepare for the worst." He say solemnly then gives me a warm smile. "But always hope for the best." His head tilts around the room. "Rely on those who rely on you." It isn't hard to understand that he means the Quint and my first instinct is to shut that down but then I remember that we are trying to move forward as a Quint. Professor Heathrow squeezes my hands back then lets go rising to his feet.

A loud voice interrupts the conversations happening around me. "It is Prince Valdis's decision if he wants to do an interview or not." Callum shouts at everyone, scolding them like a puppy.

"I agree." Dean Whyriss nods at her Prince. "The Academy has been on a social media blackout since the Flicker outbreak. Though it is your decision on how to move forward," She directs her attention to me, "I can't promise you that nothing will be leaked."

"Thank you Dean." I rise to me feet and place my finger in the Kingdom of Cures traditional greeting to show my respect to her she does the same in return. "I am not ready at this time to release a statement and I will not be taking interviews from the public." I give a firm shake of my head. The press can starve. "But I will address the Academy, if you think it would help with leaks?" I look to my Quint and see they all nod in approval. I have their support in this. "Most of the Academy already know that Atlas has pa-" My raspy voice catches and I clear my throat. "That Atlas has passed. I will do my best to clarify any misinformation the other student may have."

Dean Whyriss takes a minute to think over what I've said before replying. "Yes." She nods her head. "I think speaking with your peers would be the best course of action." She looks to Professor Heathrow who shakes his head at her. "I don't understand why you wish to remain hidden here but I will respect your decision." She turns the eTop to herself and starts clicking and typing on it then turns it back towards me. "I think the best time to hold this meeting would be this afternoon during lunch. It'll be right when core curriculum lets out and before the War and Magic curriculum starts."

"So soon?" I can hear the panic in my own voice and she gives me a kind smile.

"It is best that we get ahead of the issue." Professor Locke answers my question. "I would predict that only a small number of students have seen the news with the blackout going on. They would take it better if it came from you." Why does he have to make sense?

"Okay." It's all I can say because he is right.

Dean Whyriss collects her eTop then starts to usher her Quint towards the front door. "Everyone get some rest. Tomorrow will be a long day." Dean Whyriss is the last one to the door but she stop on the way placing her hand on my shoulder. "I'm glad that you've decided to stay with the Quint." She tilts her head to the others. "It may not have been what you wanted but I think it is what you need. I just wish that it happened in a better way."

"Me too." I say softly, the corners of my lips tilting downwards. She nods, raises her chin and follows her Quint out the door. I stare after her for a moment, wishing I could have half the confidence she does because I am going to need it in spades. The a thought hits me and I spin around to my Quint who have been waiting patiently for me to turn to them. "I've never spoken publicly before." I lock eyes with all of them rapidly, looking for an answer.

"But you've been in the tabloids hundreds of times?" Silas tilts his head.

"I've told you all a thousand times. They were staged. Minimal cast and minimal crew. There was never more than ten people there, and all were paid well for their silence." I roll my eyes. When is he going to get it?

Lucian turns towards Silas. "He was kept in that cage for his entire life. Valdis wasn't trained like we were." Then turns towards me. "Just speak only on what you need to say and know that we will be standing right behind you." His smile is dazzling. "Take strength from us."

"Okay." I let some of the stress out through a giant breath. "I'll do my best."

"Good. You got this." Lucian looks down at the crystal clock hanging over the fireplace then turns to all of us. "We should turn in. The Dean was right when she said tomorrow will be a long day."

Everyone looks stressed and tired and I can't help but feel guilty. I brought all this shit straight to their door and dumped it everywhere. Kyro follows me up the stairs and stops when I pause at my door.

"You okay?" He asks from behind me. I turn to him tilting my head back slightly to look in his gold eyes and try my best to put any of my thoughts into words but all I can manage is shaking my head. I start to tremble with all of the pent up emotion that I can't manage to strangle or bury deep enough. My hands shake the worst and I don't know what to do except drop my eyes to them and stare. Kyro gently takes my hands, steadying them. "Would you like to stay with me? Or I could stay with you if that's more comfortable? Sometimes it helps to be next to someone."

I don't allow myself to think long because I'll talk myself out of accepting what Kyro is offering. And I want it. Bad. I want someone to be there and lie to me, or tell me the truth, whatever it may be, and say that it's going to be okay. "Yours." I look away from our hands and up into his eyes. "Yours." I repeat. "My sheets are probably bloody." Kyro's eyes immediately start to glow and I can feel his healing magic rush through my body and into my spine.

"Come on." He lets go of one hand and pull me past my door with the other. We walk to the end of the hallway and he pushes his door open after it unlocks with his magical signature. I don't know what to look at first. The soft grey king sized bed with with and yellow pillows thrown about? The shelves full of red and blue medical journals with gold details? The white floor to ceiling curtains that curl and blow in the breeze coming from the open windows? The many different types of classical instruments strewn around the room? Or his two statues dedicated to the Goddess Fletinia- Chaos and phsyce, and God Flutren- Music and healing. Pictures line the walls and there's a comfortable looking couch pushed against the wall. Kyro's room looks a little cluttered but also looks loved and comforts me a little. I don't realise that he's let go of my hand until I do a full spin and come face to face with him. "Do you like it?"

"I do." A smile curls my lips up ever so slightly, Kyro smiles with me.

He walks over to the edge of his bed and takes a seat. "Good. Make yourself comfortable." He gestures around the room then pulls his waist length white hair over his shoulder and tries to put it in a braid. After his fourth attempt to tame his hair I can't help but let out a small giggle. Kyro shoots a playful glare my way and I laugh harder. "What? You're making me nervous and Callum normally braids my hair for me."

"I'm sorry." I snort. "I'm nervous too." I walk across the room and sit beside him. "Do you want me to do it?" I've braided my hair a couple times when I took my enchanted ring off and some of the more regular companion workers that I was forced to take pictures with would teach me between shots.

"Please." He groans and I move behind him.

"I'll need a-" Kyro cuts me off by handing me a comb and a hair-tie over his shoulder. "Thank you." I murmur and get to work combing through his long silky hair. I get a little lost in the motion after a while. Just running my fingers and the comb through the white strands. I'm a little jealous of his texture. I bet he never gets tangles.

"Valdis?" Kyro calls my name. His voice isn't as smooth as normal. A slight rasp breaks up the velvet his tone normally carries.

"Sorry. Your hair is just so pretty." I practically slap my hand over my mouth. Was that too feminine? Is likeing hair even a dominate female charistic? Luckily Kyro seems to ignore my little slip up. I quickly divide the hair into three even sections and start weaving the strands, tying it off at the end when finished. "Done."

Kyro pulls the braid over his shoulder and examines it. "Thank you." He looks at the crystal clock on his nightstand then turns to me. "It's getting late and we have to be up a couple hours. We should try and get some sleep."

I schooch over to the other side of the bed and help Kyro pull the sheets down. We both slip into bed and get comfortable. Me laying on my stomach and Kyro laying on his back. He looks over at me and takes in my position. "Do you always sleep on your stomach?"

The answer is simple enough. "Ever since I got the Iron Coffin. I didn't have the earring to eat away at the constant pain. Sleeping on my stomach was the comfiest way for me to get any rest." I think for a moment. "It's become a habit at this point now." I shrug my shoulders as best I can.

Kyro thinks on that for a moment before speaking. "If you could pick any position to sleep in what would it be?"

Weird question but I'll bite. "I guess it would have to be my side."

"Then come here." He holds his arms open and I gape at him.

"What?" I splutter moving off my stomach and sit on my knees looking down at him. "What do you mean?"

"You came in here with me for some comfort and I intend to deliver. I think if I hold you I'll be able to heal you throughout the night." He tilts his head. "I don't even realize how often I heal you without meaning to. I only notice later when I feel that some of my magic has depleted." He nods his head at himself then looks back at me. "So come here."

Slowly I crawl closer to him and lower myself then press against his side. I tilt my head up on his chest to look at him. His eyes glow a brilliant gold then the breeze intensifies and the lights turn off. All I can see now is a soft glow of the moon and Kyro's melted gold eyes.

I flinch slightly when I feel his hand rest on my back. He pressed his fingers into my back pushing me even closer to him. The he does the unthinkable. He slides his hand under my hoodie and starts tracing his fingers on my bare skin. A soft gasp slips from my lips when he traces his skin on my sensitive skin between the metal cuffs on my spine. His fingers freeze.

"Does that hurt?" He whispers.

I bury my face in his chest hoping he can't feel the blush heating my cheeks. "No." I whisper back because poor Kyro thinks that he hurt me.

He pauses for a minute before asking another question. "Does it feel good?"

"Yes." Kyro's finger start moving between the cuffs again. "The skin is really sensitive." His fingers move between two new cuffs and my back arches slightly. My breathing speeds up slightly.

"Must be." I can hear the smirk through his whisper.

"This isn't sleeping." I groan out and look into his slightly glowing eyes. I can see him roll his eyes.

"Your right." He flattens his hand against my back and a soft breeze disturbs the wind chimes that I didn't see earlier. Soft tinkling fill the room and I'm asleep before I can think about what just happened.

~~~

Voices wake me from the best sleep I've had in ages. "We're going to be late." Silas growls at me. How did he get in my room? And why is my pillow hard? My eyes trail around the room and it hits me that this isn't my room, it's Kyro's. I take stock of my body and notice that I'm practically laying on top of him. I notice that our legs are tangled together after I tried to launch myself away from him and fall because our legs trip me up. I land on the wooden floor with a hard thud right at Silas's feet.

"Goodmorning Valdis." Kyro calls cheerfully. "How did you sleep?"

I look up at Silas. "Just kill me now." I cover my eyes and do my best to hide my blush from everyone.

"Not today Lazy Prince." Silas answers. "We are leaving here in thirty minutes. You better be ready." He barks and instead of getting pissed at him I kick my ass into gear. I'm ready and at the door in twenty hair still dripping from my lightning fast shower.

Classes go by quickly and then there I am. Standing on a raised platform in the Quint wing ready to address the whole Academy. Two crystal screens
~~~

show my face so everyone can get a look. My Quint stands behind me and the Dean's Quint stands to the side of me. I can feel their encouragemnt through the bond before I start speaking.

"Thank you all for coming." I look into the thousands of students and continue. "I know there are some rumors going around about my family and what happend to Atlas." I take a deep breath and continue. "The only truth to these rumors is that Atlas has died." Murmurs break out over the crowd but I don't let it deter me. "For reasons I cannot specify, Atlas performed the Ritual and succedded." Now the murmurs are shouts of outrage. Calling me all kinds of names. Liar being the main one. The noise freezes me until Silas shouts into the crowd.

"SILENCE!" He roars shutting the crowd up instantly. He steps forward from behind me and places his hand on my shoulder. "Everything Prince Vladis has said is true. Myself, my Quint and the Dean's Quint can all vouch for the Prince." He looks down at me and nods to the mic.

"Thank you." I whisper to Silas. He remains by my side while I continue to speak. "I ask all of you to respect me and my Quint during the mourning period and to please refrain from talking with the press and informing them of my location while I process Atlas's death and what my next steps will be." The reactions from the crowd vary but I can't pay attention.

Pain shoots up my spine. No. No! Not here! Not now! I send warnings through the bond and stumble backwards away from the microphone. Silas turns me so my face is pressed into his chest. I trail my fingers over my left earring to activate the silencing crystal then bury my fingers into Silas combat uniform.

"Hold on Valdis. We're getting out of here." Silas mumbles into the black and white curls on the top of my head. His arms snake around me making it look like we're hugging. More arms grab me and then were moving off the stage and down some hallways. The room I'm brought into is dark but that doesn't matter. The Iron Coffin is fully activated and I lose sense of time and self.

When it finally ends I pull away from the tangle of bodies. Someone turns the lights on in the random storage closet we're apparently in and I spot a statute in the corner. The plaque on it reads 'Corintine Corvus Lustrum, Founder of Lustrum Academy of Magic and War.'

"Fucker." I growl at the statue still half delirious from the pain and ignore the concerned eyes of my Quint. Bastard shouldn't have made so many stairs.

Chapter 20: What Do You Mean Lost

V aldis Spyridon Aritiri

Monday Afternoon, Present

I wish I could say that we skipped the rest of classes after my session, but that is not the case. We finished classes using an excuse about meeting with the Dean's Quint as cover. Silas obviously hated lying but he did it because I asked him to. My Quint promises to sit right outside the door when I'm in my final two classes and a realization hits me. Sinclair isn't here. I know I had other stressful events occur but how could I possibly forget about her. She may be my very first friend and I may not know how exactly the friend thing works. But forgetting that your friend is on a dangerous mission is so not how friends friend.

I quickly whip out my eCrystal and check to see if I have any messages and start to freak a little when I don't see a notification from her. I spot Professor Heathrow immediately.

"Professor, has Sinclair been in contact with you?" I try to keep my voice even and cool. She did say that she wouldn't have much service while traveling, maybe it's just a service issue. I gnaw on my lip while I wait for Professor Heathrow to answer me.

He stands before me then sits on the ground, gesturing for me to do the same. I comply with a huff then look at him expectantly. "We briefly had contact about two hours outside of our borders then lost her signal and have not been able to reach her since." Professor Heathrow holds his hands up like that will really calm me down. "I know what you are thinking but just remember, Sinclair is trained and prepared. She will be okay and contact us tomorrow. If you don't hear from her then, then we will send a search out for her. Okay?" His eyes remain calm and I can feel his sincerity through them.

I nod my head at him reluctantly. "Okay Professor." I have a bad feeling about this.

He holds his hands out to mine and I take them. "Now we will focus on your control over your Quintessence while you tell me about what happened on your mission."

I do just that. Focus on his reaction to my recounting of what happened when Goddess Valdrestaria interacted with me and how I cleansed the souls of the Flickers. "Why did she speak to me? Guide me on how to show the lost souls to her?" I ask Professor Heathrow after I finish with my story.

Our magic still flows between us and Professor Heathrow looks at the shape and color of my soul with his glowing purple eyes. "The Goddess works in mysterious ways." He states and chuckles when I roll my eyes at him. She's a Goddess, of course she's mysterious. "I don't believe she would have shown herself to you if we had another Reaper to teach you. Most of our knowledge on them is lost. I believe she was helping to guide you." Water gathers in the Professor's eyes but he blinks the tears away. "The other Kingdoms misinterpret the Goddess of death and souls as a cruel being when in truth we know her as the kindest. The one who greets us all with open arms."

My brow furrows as my confusion keeps growing inside me. "But Flickers shouldn't have souls. It says so in all the texts. They steal souls."

"If what you say is true about you experience, and I do believe that it is, then the only thing I can think of as an explanation is that part of the soul remains when they die. Just enough for them to move and steal the soul energy from others." Professor Heathrow's head tilts, as if he is solving the hardest problem in the world. Frankly, he might be. This will shake us to the core if it is true. "Souls at their very core are magic. And through our studies we know that magic can saturate every cell. It would make sense that a being who can no longer digest nutrients would fuel themselves with the magic of others. They may even be able to steal it from the land."

"The what do they do with the rest of the soul? The term Flicker means to steal. So their name would suggest that they don't use the entire soul that they take..." Now I'm trying to solve another part of the hardest math problem. "Then where does the rest of the soul go?"

"Interesting. What makes you think that they don't use the whole soul?" I can't tell if the Professor is taking me seriously but his eyes haven't left my soul so I know that he can see that I think this is the truth.

"I think your theory on the Flickers being able to steal magic from the land is accurate." He nods at me to go on. To chase my theory down with him. "If we assume that all the reportings of disappearances are Flickers at work, then the numbers should be steadily climbing as more Flickers are made?" I finish it as a sentence. Not sure myself of where I'm going with this.

"Keep going." Professor Heathrow squeezes my hands.

"But if our intel is accurate then the numbers haven't been climbing at all." Professor Heathrow nods. "Then that would prove that the Flickers can sustain themselves off the lands magic. They don't need to sell souls at all." My eyes brighten and my magic increases, I can see slivers of other souls faintly through the walls. Students passing by the Quint wing on their way home.

"Focus." I calm myself and level out my magic. "So what does that mean Valdis?"

"It means that Flickers are intelligent and are capable of following commands. That means we have a bigger problem then we previously thought. That means, someone is controlling them."

Professor Heathrow nods gravely. "I think your theory may be spot on, and I fear that greatly." He takes his purple eyes off me and looks to the crystal clock. "Our hour here is finished. I will speak with my Quint and ask the Soul Elders to look further into this matter." Professor Heathrow goes to stand but I refuse to release him.

"Do so quietly. Only tell people you trust with your life and the lives of the people you hold most dear." My eyes lock onto his and he holds my gaze with intently. I summon my Plasma and form the Royal crest of a living bolt of lightning, something only those of royal blood can do, and place it in the palm of Professor Heathrow's hand. "If the Elders do not listen, show them my crest. I know it has no sway with them since they only serve and listen to Goddess Valdrestaria and God Valtose." My gaze travels to my feet. "But maybe they will understand the importance."

Professor Heathrow clutches the living plasma storm in his hand and nods. "I will honor you my Prince. And I believe they will listen."

"There is one more thing you must know." I shake the nerves from my mind. His safety is more important than my discomfort. "There is a traitor to the Crown."

"My Prince!" Professor Heathrow clutches my arm. Plasma sparks across his shoulders and his soul blazes in fury. "Tell me who it is and I will take care of this matter at once." He drops to his knees and holds the soul triangle out to me.

"I have no proof. Only my experience." I tell the Professor solemnly. "You know how the Court works. I'm only telling you this much because, if my theory is correct, then you might draw attention to yourself and be harmed or killed." I pause because I cannot bare for someone else to be hurt because of me. I can't bare to have another person die. I will not have another pointless sacrifice. I won't live if some dies in the same manner as Atlas. "Please rise."

"It is the job of the people to protect the Crown." Professor Heathrow states with ferocity refusing to rise to his feet. His soul still blazing.

"No." My voice is soft. The softest it has been in years. "It is the Crown's job to protect their people." I bend my knee to Professor Heathrow and guide him to his feet. I place my hands in a triangle and bow at my waist. Showing Professor Heathrow the greatest honor I can give him. "Souls be safe."

"Souls be safe." He repeats back to me, wiping a single tear from his cheek. He nods his head to me then walks out the back door.

I gather myself and head out the front door. All four Princes are propped against the wall in various position. They look like they are auditioning for a combat uniform photo shoot. I swallow the drool in my mouth before it can drip down my chin. "You all stayed?"

"We said that we would." Silas gruffs out and turns to walk out of the wing. The rest of us follow and I somehow find myself walking in the middle of our group. It feels strangely right and I allow the positive feeling flow through my body. "What took you so long to come out?" Silas's question snaps me out of my good feelings and I look around at the semi crowded path back to our Quint house.

"Not here." I sake me head and an air of seriousness surrounds us. We remain quiet until we get back to the house. I find myself sandwiched between Callum and Kyro while Lucian and Silas sit on the couch in front of me. I tell them what I can about my lesson with the Professor. Which is basically everything except about the part involving the Goddess.

"Do you trust Professor Heathrow and his Quint?" Lucian asks.

"I haven't talked much with Professor Locke, Alister, or Julia." I rub my hands over my face aggressively. "But I do trust Professor Heathrow and Dean Whyriss." I look up at Lucian. "I'm familiar with Heathrow's soul and I've trusted the Dean since I met her." I tilt my head from side to side. "I trust their judgement and the Gods wouldn't have paired them together if their morals didn't align. Right?"

"Right." Lucian confirms my question. "They may have different actions but their core morals will be similar."

A hand pulls my chin so I'm face to face with Kyro. "Something is still troubling you. I can feel a spike in your cortisol levels."

"Dude, just say stress." Callum calls over my shoulder pressing into my side.

Kyro rolls his eyes. "What else is stressing you?"

"Sinclair hasn't contacted me." I pull out my eCrystal and show our message thread. The only activity is me asking if she's okay at breakfast, lunch, and dinner since she left. My messages get more hysterical as the days pass.

A firm hand starts to massage my hip and I know it's Callum. "When is she supposed to arrive at her location?"

"Tomorrow morning." I can see the frowns on most of their faces. They don't think there is an issue. But I do. "I know the service is spotty but Sinclair should have had some signal to send a message through in the past 32 hours." I pull my face out of Kyro's hand. "She's important to me." I whisper the last words because fear crawls around in my chest. It's scary to care about some.

A loud sigh sounds from across the room turning my gaze to Silas. "I'll contact my scouts." He pulls his own eCrystal from his pocket. "Do you know the route she is taking?" Silas doesn't look up from his typing.

I perk up instantly and start doing my own typing. I find the Dean's contact info and send her a text rapidly. She gets back to my almost instantly, sending me the exact route Sinclair used and her estimated location based off of time. I try to pull up Silas number and pause. Psycho. Stalker. Ghost. Demon. Shit. I still don't know who is who. Deciding the deal I made with Callum isn't more important than Sinclair's life, I create a group chat and send it to all of them. Everyone's eCrystals chime at the same time. Callum chuckles and leans close to my ear. "Still don't know who is who?" He whispers sending tingles down my spine.

"Not yet, it's only been a little more than a day." I turn my head towards him then move my head back quickly. He was much closer than I thought he would be. "I have until the end of the week to figure it out."

He leans forward more making me lean back against Kyro. "I hope you don't." Callum moves away from me leaving my head spinning and cheeks slightly pink. I can feel Kyro chuckling to himself and sit back upright in my own seat.

"I sent the route over to some of my scouts. They will track along her route and try to meet up with her. I should have some info for you in the next eight hours." Silas finally looks up from his eCrystal and tracks the blush along my cheeks and ears. He between Kyro and Callum a couple times before focusing back at me with a slight down turn to his lips.

"What am I supposed to do for eight hours?"

"I have a couple things in mind." Callum whispers under his breath but I hear him anyway. The slight pink to my cheeks has turned bright red. Dick.

It's Silas's turn to roll his eyes. "Eat, study, sleep." He stands and starts walking towards his room on the ground floor. "I don't care."

I call out to him just before he leaves the room, he pauses but doesn't turn to look at me. "Thank you." He nods his head then leaves the room. Kyro excuses himself and walks after Silas. Lucian and Callum are next. I'm the last to leave the living room and head up to my own bedroom but I pause in the doorway. After seeing Kyro's room mine looks bland in comparison. It looks like I never left my cage at all. I decide to take a long shower and change into some comfortable black sweats before taking my books and eTop into the living room to complete my assignment for today.

I'm just getting comfortable when a notification comes in on my eCrystal. I fling my pen across the room in my attempt to get the slippery bitch out of my pocket. I'm slightly disappointed that it isn't Sinclair but I'm still happy with who is messaging me.

Sir Howin: I think I found a lead in the papers you brought me from the compound where you were kept. It may not be much but it looks like you weren't only person he did this to. I'll follow up more but just wanted to keep you updated. I think this could be our break.

Me: Thank you for informing me. If he has done this to other people and we can get proof then I won't wait till my coronation. I'll kill him the moment the evidence is solid. Happy hunting Sir Howin. Souls be safe.

Sir Howin: Souls be safe.

It doesn't take me long to lose myself in my assignments. These are answers that I can solve, but I find boredom and tiredness creeping up on me. I'm out fast asleep before I can put my new pen down.

I jolt wide awake when a hand trails over my spine sending tingles through my whole body. Lucians braids clink together when he leans down. "Dinner is ready." He holds a hand out to me and I take it. A piece of paper sticks to my face and I rip it away and place it back on one of the books I have strew around the living room. When I look at Lucian his hand is covering his mouth and his shoulders are shaking.

"Yeah yeah. Laugh it up." I shake my head at him and grin. I sober quickly. "It there any news?"

"Not yet, but I assume you will be the first person Silas tells." He pulls me by my hand and leads me to the kitchen. "Lets eat."

Dinner goes by quickly. A sense of comradery settles between underlined by my anxiety. After we was dishes everyone goes to bed where I find myself staring at my blank room. Instead of going to sleep I walk over to the window and climbing out of it. Something out here is calling to me. I decide to sit in the tree and wait for whatever the answer is.

It comes moments later when I hear the pattering of raindrops landing on leaves and lights streak across the sky followed by low rumbles. A storm is here. I can feel the energy pulsing in the air and I climb down from my perch. The small clearing of the back yard will do nicely. I walk to the center and lay on my back, even though it pains me, so I can watch God Valtose, God of storms and forgiveness, at work.

The seasons are starting to change and what was once warm will now be cold.

The storm picks up in energy and the lightning comes in quicker. I can feel it vibrate through the earth when it connects. The roar of thunder is almost deafening coming only a second or two after the lightning and I know with certainty that the storm is almost right on top of me. But I cannot move. All I can do is bask in the glory. Rain pelts my skin, feeling like tiny needles stabbing me all over but the pain isn't bad. It isn't even enough for the enchanted earring to dull.

The cold seeps through my metal spin and soaks my entire body. Even my bones are cold. I couldn't tell you how long I lay out here. All I know is that here is where I belong. Among the storm. Lightning strikes closer to me and it sounds like a bomb is going off. I want to touch it. I want to feel that power and see if it can feel me back. I have no idea what it would do. All I know is that it might work. Work for what? Hmmm. Just that it would work. Almost.

I see the energy coming down from the sky and I can feel the energy beneath me eager to join. I roll away at the last second too afraid to try and lightning strikes three feet away from me. The Quint needs me. I can feel the residual energy through the ground soak into my cells and I feel lighter. Like I just got the best hug from a friend I haven't seen in a long time. I pull myself up to my knees and bow. "May the storm rage and the heart heal." I swear the rumble of thunder answers me back but I could just be crazy. I was about to let lightning strike me.

Shouts pull me from my weirdness and I walk to the back door. I open it and soak the floor instantly. Footsteps rumble down the stairs and then all four Princes are pulling me in every direction I can feel concern flow through the bonds and I rip myself away from them and smooth down my soaking wet sweat set. "I'm fine."

"What the fuck were you doing outside?" Silas grabs me by the shoulders and shakes me. Rude.

It takes my rattled brain a second to answer him. "It's the storm." I gesture to the glass door as best as I can.

"We can see that there's a storm. Why were you outside in it?" He snarls at me. Gods, why is he so worked up right now.

I pull my arms away from him. "No, not a storm. The storm." Silas looks at me like I'm crazy and I guess that I am. I didn't realize what day it was until now. "I can almost guarantee that everyone with Plasma at this Academy is outside right now. It's the storm that marks the beginning of fall." They all still look at me like I'm crazy. Maybe I am. "It's a Kingdom of Souls thing." They all think for a moment before some memory they have of Atlas must be triggered and they all nod. "That isn't important right now. Why were you looking for me?"

Silas takes a deep breath before pulling me over to the couch and sitting with me. "My scouts found Sinclair's EMC three hours from here. They didn't find Sinclair."

Panic grips me. "Three hours from here? That would mean that she's been missing for 40 hours. She disappeared right after she told me she was leaving service range. Forty hours." Warm hands grab me and I tilt my head back to see Lucian providing me strength.

"There's more." Silas locks his eyes on mine. "They found the bodies of five Flickers."

A wail leaves my lips and I crumble to the floor. "She was taken. I was supposed to prote-" My sentence is broken as pain shoots up my metal spine. "No." Regent Lukadious's timing is absolute shit.

Chapter 21: Everything We Can Do

V aldis Spyridon Aritiri

Tuesday Morning, Present

Everyone held me through my torture session. Kyro brought me to his room again and held me through the night as I cried for my friend. Another body joined us as I slept fitfully. I wake with Kyro curled against my back and Callum's blond curls tucked under my chin. He smells of fresh water and frost. Delicious.

His arms band around my waist while Kyro's band across my chest. My leg is thrown over Callum's waist and my fingers curl through is hair. Maybe I should start tucking a sock in my boxers. These men are getting awfully close to figuring out that I don't have a dick and I may not actually be a boy. Kyro shift against my back pressing me closer into Callum. My mind wants to go to inappropriate places but I understand what these two men are giving me. Comfort.

I try to peek over my shoulder and over Kyro to see what time it is without either of them waking. I am unsuccessful at seeing the time. Soft chuckles bring my gaze to the bedroom door where Lucian is leaning against the frame.

"I was wondering where Callum went last night." Lucian whispers. "Now I know." His smile is soft, warm. Do they sleep in the same room often?

"Sorry." My cheeks heat. Callum tightens his arms around me and he presses his face further into my chest. "I guess Kyro called in reinforcements." I try to shrug my shoulders but Kyro tightens himself around me. My eyes fall back on Lucian. "I can't breathe."

Lucian looks like he's about to grab them both my the scruff and throw them. "No." I whisper shout. "Let them sleep. I think I kept them up most of the night." Lucian gives a nod then grabs me by my ankles. "What are yo-" He yanks me, hard. I slide out of the foot of the bed and am now sitting on my ass staring up into Lucians grinning face.

"They're still sleeping, lets go." He pulls me up and we follow each other out and down the stairs. Silas is sitting on the couch by the fireplace with three steaming mugs. The sun is just rising and there's a fire burning. I sit opposite Silas and Lucian falls into the seat next to me. Silas slides the two mugs towards us and I take mine gladly. I pull out my eCrystal and call Sir Howin.

"Good morning my Prince." He answers on the second ring, sleep heavy in his voice. "What can I do for you?"

"Sinclair has been taken. I need you to get me her father's contact information so I can inform him." My voice is heavy but I did my crying yesterday. Today I need to be strong. I need to be strong for Sinclair.

Sir Howin is quiet for a few moments and I can hear soft clicking in the background. "It's going to take me a moment to find Major Kairos. He went underground after Regent Lukadious took over. I'll send you a message when I figure it out." More clicks sound. "I also don't have an update on where the Flickers are taking the people matching your age and without Sinclair it doesn't look like I'll be able to figure it out but I'll keep crunching the numbers and will get back to you as soon as I can."

I take a small breath as disappointment swells in my body, then guilt. It isn't Sinclair's or Sir Howin's fault that we can't figure this out. "Thank you. Souls be safe." I end the call after he repeats my words. I sagg into the couch and take a sip and hum. The coffee is good. There's so much I need to get done and I feel like time is running out. So many people are getting hurt and I'm just sitting here. Huge swells of negative emotions flood my emotions and I can feel sparks on my fingers and shoulders. A hand lands on my thigh bringing me back to the present. Lucian and Silas are both staring at me. "Sorry." I take another sip of my coffee.

"Sir Howin?" Silas asks. His orange eyes staring at my hands.

I set the mug on the coffee table and tuck my legs under my body. "Yes. He's getting me in touch with Sinclair's father. I have to let him know what has happened." I choke down the tears that want to break past my mantra of being strong today.

"Major Kairos?" Lucian pulls his hand away from my thigh and rests his arm on the back of the couch behind me. "Didn't he disappear after your parents..." He doesn't finish his sentence.

"Died." I fill in the blank for him. "You can say it. I never knew them." I give him a small smile. "And yes. Major Kairos went underground after, but Sinclair says he's doing well." I rub my bottom lip with my finger. "That's all I know about him."

"From what my parents told me about him, he was a great and honorable man. He opposed Regent Lukadious taking over until you and Atlas came of age. That's what got him demoted." Silas shrugs his shoulders. "If Sir

Howin can't turn anything up then you should speak with Callum. His family was also fond of the Major."

I give a nod then look at the crystal clock. A sigh leaves my body and I get to my feet. "We're gonna be late for Combat." We all break apart and get ready.

Callum has burritos ready for us when we meet back up at the front door. We walk together to the training yard a comfortable silence falling on us all. I bump shoulders with Callum on the way. "Thank you for staying with me."

"We can have a sleepover anytime you want cuddle bug." He winks at me and my face heats.

"Cuddle bug?" I shake my head.

"Yeah cuddle bug, you latched onto me as soon as I laid down." He smirks. "Grabbed onto my hair and wouldn't let me go." He runs a hand through his hair. "I mean, I like my hair being pulled but you were a little rough Val."

I choke on my burrito. "Stop talking. I did not." I think back to this morning and my hand indeed was in Callum's hair when I woke up. I quicken my pace but I can feel him behind me. I can feel when he leans close to my ear and whispers.

"It's okay. You can pull my hair anytime you like."

Thankfully we get to class so I don't have to give his comment a response. Though my heated cheeks are all the response he needs.

Classes go as smoothly as can be. If you include my paranoia about being tortured at anytime and waiting on Sir Howin to give me Major Kairos's contact information. It isn't until lunch time that the first thing happens. I had just ordered my food when I felt the first pulse. Lucian was the closest to me and doesn't ask a single question before he's pulling me from my seat and finding the closest empty room for me. I tug on my left earring and hell breaks loose. Everyone is there and the session is the most painful one yet.

Blood seeps from my eyes, nose and ears. The only brightside is that this session has been the shortest one yet. Once everyone is sure that it's over we all take a collective breath. Kyro rips up my black combat shirt and dark purple compression shirt before I've totally collected myself. "What are you doing?" I hiss out still feeling the phantom pains. I hiss again again when Kyro's cold fingers trail between the metal cuffs, his healing magic following his fingers.

"There are black lines in your skin branching off the cuffs." Kyro speaks in a low tone. "It looks like your being poisoned or infected." I feel more of his healing magic flow through my back. "Silas." I can hear some shuffling behind me then gasp when I feel a wave of healing magic take over my body. Silas must be giving Kyro power. It must go on for five minutes before it stops. "I can't heal it." Kyro pants sounding crushed.

My head drops low on my shoulders pressing my forehead against Lucian's chest. "Are you okay?" He asks.

I nod my head. "It was bound to kill me one day. I just didn't think it would be like this." Then another idea falls through my head. "I think it might actually be burning through my nerve endings."

Callum gives me a grave look and takes a slow breath in before speaking again. "We will figure something out." He says scooting closer. "We've got ten minutes before class starts." He pushes some togo boxes towards everyone. "Eat quickly." No one says a word, we all just start stuffing our faces and patting each other on the back when we start to choke.

We all part ways for our respective classes and the day continues like nothing happened. My respect grows for my fellow classmates, as not one of them has uttered a word to anyone about me being at the academy.

It's when I'm walking through the doors to my extra lessons when Sir Howin sends me a text with Major Kairos's number. Professor Heathrow clears his throat and I realize that I'm standing frozen in the doorway. "Is something the matter Prince Valdis?" He tilts his head to the side and studies me.

"Is there any update on Sinclair?" I ask hesitantly, scared that he will have no information for me.

"I'm afraid nothing has turned up so far." He tilts his head down in a bow.

I step fully into the room and our purple eyes meet before I speak again. "My knight has found Major Kairos's eCrystal frequency. I have to update him on Sinclair." I inhale, hold for a few seconds then exhale. "I don't know what I'm supposed to say?"

"Major Kairos and I were good friends before he went underground." Professor Heathrow gets a faraway look in his eyes as if he's recalling past times, better times. "I could speak with him for you? It would be nice to hear his voice." He offers and it warms my heart but is shake my head.

"You are kind to offer but I need to be the one to make this call. I was the one who sent her on this mission." I raise my head and Professor Heathrow gives me a curious look. "I must take responsibility for my actions."

Professor Heathrow pulls me fully into the room before looking around the room. His eyes glow a brilliantly bright purple and I know he is using his quintessence to ensure we are alone before speaking. "What do you mean you sent her on her mission?"

"It is true that fifth years can meet up with different military units in the five kingdoms but Sinclair was using that as a ruse to investigate some of the disappearances around the border of the Kingdom of Runes for me." I whisper to him. "She was only there under my order."

"Do you know something about the disappearances that the heads of the Academy do not?" His eyes widen and his hand grips my shoulder tightly.

I shake my head. "I have no proof so I shall not speak on the matter. Not even in theory."

Professor Heathrow straightens. "I understand." He pauses and rubs his face aggressively. "How much danger is Sinclair in?"

My breath hitches and I take a second to calm myself. "Grave. She is in Grave danger."

"Then you must invite Major Kairos into your inner circle." Professor Heathrow is pacing back and forth now. "He is a brilliant man and I know he will want to do everything in his power to get his daughter back. So for the moment. Your goals align." He pauses his pacing to stare at me. "When you speak with him you must be clear with him." Professor Heathrow heads to the door and opens it. "We will cut our lesson for the day. Go somewhere private where you can speak with him freely." He gives me a soft smile. "And try not to take any of his harshness personally. He loves his daughter very very much."

I nod to Professor and leave the room, heading out of the wing and out of the Academy. I don't stop until I stand before Atlas's statue in the Warrior's Meadow. I engage my quintessence and scan the area, when I'm satisfied that no souls are around I call Major Kairos.

"Who is this? How did you get this frequency?" A deep gruff voice answers.

I clear my throat before speaking. "This is Prince Valdis Spyridon Aritiri of the Kingdom of Souls. Am I speaking with Major Kairos?"

"What business do you have with me boy?" He growls into the phone.

I suck in a shaky inhale and steel myself. "I need your help. Sinclair has gone missing."

"Are the details classified? My line is secure but is your's?" His tone goes from grouchy old man to a seasoned veteran instantly.

"I cannot be certain that my line is secure though very few people have this number." I convey back to him.

I can hear him take in a slow breath. "Send me a private location were we can meet and discuss what has happened." He hangs up before I can answer him. I send a message to Sir Howin and then send the longitude and latitude of the cabin where Sir Howin has been working.

'I will be there in 1 hour.' Is all Major Kairos sends back.

Shit. How am I supposed to get out there? Sinclair has been my ride this whole time.

I rub my forehead in irritation realizing I have to message the rest of my quint.

'I need an EMC I have a meeting with Major Kairos in town in less than an hour.'

Psycho- 'Do you even know how to drive?'

Ghost- 'We have one you can borrow.'

Stalker- 'I assume you need someone to drive you?'

Demon- 'Do you want us to go with you?'

Me- 'Sinclair showed me how to drive. No I don't need you guys to come with me. Where is the EMC at?'

Ghost- 'I can have the faculty bring it to you. Where are you located right now?'

Me- 'Thank you. I'm at the Warrior's Meadow.'

Demon- 'Are you okay?'

Ghost- 'Head to the road, the EMC should be there in a few minutes.'

Me- 'I'm okay. Thank you for the EMC, I'll tell you all how the meeting goes when I get back.'

I don't wait for a response and head to the road. A young faculty member greets me and gives me the keys to a sleek looking EMC but it looks normal enough that I shouldn't be noticed. I hop in the drivers seat and make a bumpy journey to the cabin. I do almost smoke a few trees on the way out there, I did say I could drive, not that I was a good driver.

When I pull up to the cabin an EMC that looks very similar to Sinclairs, only larger, sits to the side of the cabin. Major Kairos is here. Steadying my mind I park the EMC and walk onto the back patio. A man with long golden hair pulled back in an intricate braid that looks like a mohawk stands from one of the rocking chairs. His form keeps getting taller the more he straightens from is sitting position. Major Kairos is quite possible the largest man I've ever seen. Fuck.

"Souls be safe." I place my hands in the traditional greeting and give him the lowest bow I can bestow. "I'm am Prince Valdis, thank you fo-"

"You can go ahead and cut the shit Princess, I was there when you were born." He says in his gruff voice and I can feel the bass all the way down to my toes. "I will not have us start this meeting off on lies and half truths."

I give a shaky nod and remove the enchanted ring from my left thumb and place it in my pocket. The glamour fades quickly. My breasts and hips fill out, my waist thins, my shoulders narrow, my jaw softens, and my hair tumbles past my waist in black and white curls. "I am Princess Valdis Spyridon Aritiri of the Kingdom of Souls, first born heir to the throne and rightful ruler." My voice is not as strong as I wanted it to be but my shoulders are straight and my knees don't shake. "I wish the circumstances were different but I am honored to meet you Major Kairos."

"I wish the circumstances were different as well Princess." Plasma dances across his shoulders but with a clench of his fists it dissipates. "Now, tell me about my daughter." He commands, everybit the legendary Major from the histories I've been told. Then he softens and all I see is a scared father. "Please." He whispers.

"She was doing me a favor." I choke down the sob that wants to escape. Shaking my head to get myself back under control I start again. "She was investigating some of the most recent disappearances for me." I shake my hands in the air. "A pattern appeared, one only my Knight and I knew to look for. Sinclair was apart of my investigation since around the beginning."

"Did you order my daughter to go on this mission?" Major Kairos asks in a low voice.

The tears do come now. "Never." A sob escapes and I choke more back. "I would never order my best friend to go on this wild goose chase. I would never order anyone to do this. The only thing I have ordered from anyone is their silence but only when required." I wipe the irritating fluids from my eyes and nose. "According to the patterns and data, not a single soul should have been on her route. She was supposed to be safe."

A hand rests on my shoulder and turns me. Sir Howin's kind eyes meet mine and he softly pulls me into a warm embrace. It only succeeds in making me cry harder. "Calm now Princess. Let's invite Major Kairos inside and show him everything we have."

I hiccup in Sir Howin's chest. "Everything?"

"Yes, everything. He was your father's right hand for a reason." Sir Howin ushers us inside the cabin and has me sit on the couch. A teacup is placed in my hand and a soft blanket around my shoulders. I can see Major Kairos look around at all the boxes and loose papers.

"What is all this?" He waves his hand around the room.

"It's everything we've been able to find on Regent Lukadious and those he associates with." Sir Howin states without so much as a twitch.

Major Kairos takes a moment to think about Sir Howins words and mine from earlier. "You think the Regent plays a part in all of the disappearances?" I nod my head and he continues. "And you're going to do what exactly?"

"I'm going to find concrete evidence then I'm going to execute him and take my rightful place on the throne." The strength I wished I had had earlier is now present in my voice. Major Kairos's head snaps to me, his eyes full of shock. "He will pay for everything he has done to me and my people." Plasma dances across my shoulders and in my eyes.

"What has he done to you Princess?" Major Kairos steels his expression as if waiting for a blow.

"He has taken everything from me Major. Since the day I was born, all the Regent has done is take." The coldness in my voice chill even myself. "I am going to rip his spine out with my bare hands."

Major Kairos's purple eyes start to glow and I let down the guards placed around my soul. I bare my pain to the Major and he inhales sharply before darting to an empty box and throwing up. Once he has taken care of the box outside he returns and faces me. "Start from the beginning."

www.ingramcontent.com/pod-product-compliance
Lightning Source LLC
Chambersburg PA
CBHW070353200726
48294CB00003B/893